A steady stream
chewed into Ascherreld's table

Even as the first gunner's clip ran dry, a second attacker fell in at his side. Screams punctuated the roar of the submachine gun as the bullets pursued the dodging bodyguards struggling to bring their weapons into play.

Bolan's .44 cleared leather as he rolled into the aisle, his two Magnum rounds putting the subgunner down permanently. Then the Executioner was up and battling through the human tide driven by sudden fear toward the entrance. He elbowed the man closest to him and the guy stumbled, allowing Bolan to break through the line.

The first assassin lowered his recharged weapon as Bolan settled the big Desert Eagle in a two-handed Weaver's grip. More subguns joined the first two, driving the Russian agents to cover.

The warrior pulled two shots in rapid fire, not bothering with actual sighting, relying on his honed instincts. Both shots struck the man below the jaw.

Then Bolan felt a red hot stinger stab into his neck. Unable to maintain his balance, he went down, blood sliding down his back and shoulder.

MACK BOLAN®

The Executioner

DON PENDLETON'S

THE EXECUTIONER®

FEATURING MACK BOLAN®

FAST STRIKE

A GOLD EAGLE BOOK FROM

WORLDWIDE®

TORONTO • NEW YORK • LONDON
AMSTERDAM • PARIS • SYDNEY • HAMBURG
STOCKHOLM • ATHENS • TOKYO • MILAN
MADRID • WARSAW • BUDAPEST • AUCKLAND

First edition April 1993

ISBN 0-373-61172-2

Special thanks and acknowledgment to
Mel Odom for his contribution to this work.

FAST STRIKE

Peace cannot be kept by force. It can only be
achieved by understanding.

—Albert Einstein

It's a fool's dream to think a handful of people can
achieve world peace. If it's ever going to be achieved,
it's going to take just that—the world.

—Mack Bolan

THE
MACK BOLAN®
LEGEND

Nothing less than a war could have fashioned the destiny of the man called Mack Bolan. Bolan earned the Executioner title in the jungle hell of Vietnam.

But this soldier also wore another name—Sergeant Mercy. He was so tagged because of the compassion he showed to wounded comrades-in-arms and Vietnamese civilians.

Mack Bolan's second tour of duty ended prematurely when he was given emergency leave to return home and bury his family, victims of the Mob. Then he declared a one-man war against the Mafia.

He confronted the Families head-on from coast to coast, and soon a hope of victory began to appear. But Bolan had broken society's every rule. That same society started gunning for this elusive warrior—to no avail.

So Bolan was offered amnesty to work within the system against terrorism. This time, as an employee of Uncle Sam, Bolan became Colonel John Phoenix. With a command center at Stony Man Farm in Virginia, he and his new allies—Able Team and Phoenix Force—waged relentless war on a new adversary: the KGB.

But when his one true love, April Rose, died at the hands of the Soviet terror machine, Bolan severed all ties with Establishment authority.

Now, after a lengthy lone-wolf struggle and much soul-searching, the Executioner has agreed to enter an ''arm's-length'' alliance with his government once more, reserving the right to pursue personal missions in his Everlasting War.

1

September, 1990

Mack Bolan confirmed the tail as he passed the historic corner of Zimmerstrasse and Friedrichstrasse. The twin headlight beams stayed locked on to his rearview mirror as he made the turn onto Unter den Linden. Automatically he swept his gaze across the terrain with a soldier's eye. The small Miafiori 1600 he'd found waiting for him at Tegel airport wasn't designed with rapid getaways in mind.

He steered and shifted gears, his attention drawn momentarily to the action below the Brandenburger Tor. Police cruisers had surrounded a parked car as an ambulance with its Klaxons blaring crept through the stalled traffic.

The warrior rolled his window down slightly to let the night air and the noise in. The commands and voices were in German. His knowledge of the language was geared more for survival than for understanding police matters. Someone was dead, killed, and that was all he knew.

When he glanced up he saw that his tail had closed the distance to two car-lengths. The traffic jam forced him to slow. He watched the doors on the trailing

Lada with interest, wondering if the men inside would try to take him in the confusion.

Through Aaron Kurtzman's computers at Stony Man, Hal Brognola had arranged the papers he carried. It was definitely a hush-rush, the big Fed had said during their brief conversation, but he'd said little else. Bolan had been in the Bahamas finishing cashing in his interest in a cocaine supplier's accounts when he'd returned Brognola's call. That had been less than sixteen hours ago. Even with the ID in place, there'd been no way to bring weapons in from London. He was alone and unarmed in a land still raw and torn from the shadow of forty years of cold war. And he was being trailed by an unknown enemy.

Gray-uniformed border guards spilled from trucks ahead of the traffic congested along the street. The warrior heard their hoarse shouted commands to the motorists as they began directing traffic and searching cars. Flashlights shone into vehicles indiscriminately as two-man teams swept down the stalled lanes. One directed the flashlight and kept a hand on his holstered pistol, while the other carried a Heckler & Koch MP-5 submachine gun at the ready.

Bolan waited patiently, keeping his attention on the car behind the BMW at his rear bumper. He logged the time automatically—9:27 p.m. He readied his papers and visa as he waited.

The ambulance made its way through the police cars and stopped beside the stalled Trabant. Bolan got an impression of blood-covered bodies on the ground as the lights flickered across them.

Gearing down, he eased his foot off the clutch and rolled forward at the border guard's wave. He came to a smooth stop, extended his papers through the open window and said, "Good evening."

The guard was young. So was his companion. The one holding the flashlight swept it across the interior of the Miafiori. "Good evening," he replied as he turned his attention to the papers.

"What's the trouble?" Bolan asked. Before the wall had crumbled between the two Germanys, such a question in East Berlin easily could have earned him a night with the Volkspolizei. Now, though, the lack of curiosity could have drawn attention to him.

"There has been a murder," the guard replied as he flipped through the pages and took a closer look at the passport photo.

As Bolan checked the rearview mirror, one of the men in the tailing car got out and advanced to the window of the BMW. There was a brief discussion, then the woman driver of the BMW tugged her steering wheel hard to the right, causing the power-steering unit to squeak. The man continued forward with his hands in his pockets, coming to a stop at the rear bumper of the Miafiori. "Who was the murdered man?"

The young guard looked up over his perusal of the papers. "An economist. Why do you ask?"

"Check the work section in the papers," Bolan advised. "You'll see that I'm employed by a television news station."

The guard confirmed it. "I'm sorry, but at this time I can give out no more details without departmental authorization." He handed the papers back and waved him through.

Bolan eased away from the roadblock, gaining speed as he continued down Unter den Linden. Assuming he couldn't flush the tail in the car, his only option was on foot in the darkness. He'd already selected his site from the mental maps he'd prepared for his penetration into East Berlin.

He watched the rearview mirror as the man beside the border guards waved frantically. Blue splashes from the police car lights washed over the man, giving him a surrealistic look.

The BMW pulled over at once, rolling up onto the curb. The guard carrying the H&K MP-5 leveled it immediately, then dropped it apologetically as the man showed him something in his hand. The tail pulled forward with a screech of rubber, and the man got in the back. As it passed through the field of light given off by the other waiting cars, the Executioner identified it as a dark Lada 1200 with at least four men inside.

He worked the clutch and gearshift, making the engine whine as he sped up. The Lada whipped into view around the corner as he guided the Miafiori across Berlin's Red Square, cut through the light traffic around Alexanderplatz and roared onto Lenin Allee.

Swallowed by the monolithic proportions of the street's double row of shadowy apartment buildings and shops, Bolan abandoned the Miafiori at the second side street. He left the car turned sideways to block the entrance, then threw the keys into a row of small hedges.

Bolan wore a dark turtleneck, jeans and black runners, and he used the shadows like the pro that he was.

His forward momentum slowed, and he became silent when he heard the Lada skid to a stop behind the Miafiori. The driver brought the headlights around to shine down the narrow street. Shadows were chased away immediately by the bright lights. The Executioner vanished with them, unseen by his pursuers.

TWENTY MINUTES LATER Bolan was sure he'd eluded the men who'd been following him. He'd watched from the top of an apartment house as two more Ladas joined the first. One team searched the abandoned Miafiori while the others fanned out along the streets. All were dressed in street clothes, leading the warrior to believe they were members of the Volkspolizei rather than the border guards. Instead of answering questions, the observation only focused his curiosity on why the Vopos would be interested in his cover identity.

The safehouse address Brognola had given him in code during the phone conversation was a ground-floor apartment near the corner of Lenin Allee and Landsburger Allee opposite the large cemetery. A walk-up shop over the apartment advertised jewelry and engraving.

Like all the other apartments and stores in the area, this one had the look and feel of Moscow gingerbread-style architecture. The residences looked cramped and uncomfortable, as if they froze in the winter and sweltered in the summer.

Bolan crossed the street with his head down, relying on his peripheral vision and hearing to warn him of any danger. The area seemed deserted at that time of night, and only a handful of cars had passed him as he'd doubled back on his route to make sure he wasn't being followed.

He walked by the apartment the first time, like a man on his way to somewhere else. He logged the absence of lights, the spinning arms of the plastic windmill in the window box amid a cluster of artificial flowers and the name plaque indicating the Conradts lived there.

A block down, the Executioner immersed himself in the shadows again. Something was wrong. It was nothing his five physical senses could quantify. But that sixth sense he'd developed in the jungles of Vietnam scratched at his mind with a low, threatening buzz.

He retreated down the alley for a brief recon, discovering there was no back way into the building that didn't involve going through another residence first. The fire escape that ran alongside the building had a loose railing. He tugged it free on the second jerk and took it with him, holding it like a cane instead of a weapon.

Senses still tingling from the unidentified warning, Bolan stopped in front of the safehouse door and tried the knob. The door was unlocked and pushed open easily. He slipped inside and closed the door behind him, gripping the wrought-iron bar loosely like a baseball player stepping up to the plate.

The living room was small, filled with a sparse array of old and overstuffed furniture. He waited until his eyes adjusted to the interior gloom before attempting to move. Using his pen-flash in quick bursts, he took in the arrangement of the furniture and the spread of pictures covering the walls. Most of them were of small children with innocent smiles.

He moved through the room, walking past the dining room with its lilac candles and deep-seated aroma of bratwurst and sauerkraut. He found the first bodies in the kitchen.

The warrior dropped to his knees as he listened, checking the old woman's wrist. The body was still warm, but there was no pulse. Bolan hadn't expected any after seeing the long slice that ran from ear to ear across her throat. The old man's death had come just as suddenly. A loose collection of bullet holes had ripped open his chest.

Bolan moved on. There was nothing he could do for the dead.

He paused at the open-faced cupboard to his left. His searching fingers found the hidden latch, and he released it. The whole cupboard swung outward on silent hinges, revealing darkness and the first few steps of a narrow wooden stairway. He used the pen-flash as the smells of cordite and sudden death filled his nostrils. He had no illusions about the probable condition of the three CIA agents who were supposed to be waiting to brief him.

The yellow ellipse of the pen-flash found the first man at the bottom of the stairs. He was on his back. Most of his face had been shot away.

Bolan stepped over the body, finding the corpses of the other two men against the far wall. The round table in the center of the tiny room glared white where bullets had scored chips from its surface. A coal-oil lantern hung from the ceiling. He lit it and put the pen-flash away. The scent of the burning coal oil helped diffuse some of the congested smell of death.

Spray-painted propaganda and slogans covered the cinder-block walls. Some of them were in English. All of the ones Bolan could make out had to do with condemning American oppression.

He took a pistol from the nearest corpse—a Heckler & Koch Model P-9S 9 mm automatic—broke it open and inspected it. It was normally a good gun, originally designed for the West German police. Someone had broken the firing pin in the one he held. He put it on the table and checked the other two. Same thing.

Bolan knew he'd stepped into a trap. The scuff of shoe leather across the wooden floor in the living room let him know its jaws were closing.

"WHAT HAVE YOU found out about Krispin Doeker?"

Firenze Falkenhayn answered the male voice without turning around. "He is dead." She moved through the crowd thronging the Brandenburger Tor, finding gaps that made René Girauld work to keep up with her. She didn't like meeting here, didn't like staying this close to one of her mission's objectives. The fact that one of the multilayers of duplicity had already been penetrated was something she liked even less. Girauld she liked least of all.

"Don't play games with me, girl," Girauld warned. His voice, though barely a whisper, carried the full weight of his authority.

Falkenhayn turned to him. She was strikingly beautiful and knew it. This night her long blond curls were tucked neatly under a short-brimmed hat. Nonprescription lenses took away the impact of her fog-gray eyes. A loose blouse softened the curves, while a long, shapeless skirt took away all but the delicately turned ankles. She'd learned to hide her charms at the same time she'd been taught how to use them with the deadly efficiency of a machine pistol.

"You are the one playing games here," she replied, snugging her hands into her gloves again. "Do you concern yourself with the risk of exposure I am running by being here tonight?"

Girauld was a small, colorless man in a porkpie hat and tan trench coat. He blended into the crowd around him effortlessly. The whirling blue flare of the Vopos' lights tinted his brief smile a soft sapphire. *"Mais oui!"*

"Speak German."

Girauld stood there, his hands buried in his trench coat pockets. "Of course. Forgive me."

She gazed at him with no emotion, then returned her attention to the ambulance. The workers were loading Doeker's body. The September wind cut through the crowd, making her pull the long coat more tightly about her body.

"What have your American contacts had to say about his death?" Girauld asked.

"I have not heard from them tonight. This event is less than an hour old."

"I cannot believe they do not know. They were keeping a loose watch over him, as well."

"Perhaps they are having problems of their own," Falkenhayn suggested.

One of the Vopos stepped forward to shut the door of the ambulance with a loud whump of displaced air.

Other members of the Volkspolzei worked the area of the actual assassination. Occasionally light sparkled from a spent brass casing as it was added to an evidence bag. The border guards still searched cars, cycling through the onlookers and checking papers, falling back on the standbys they had relied upon for years to keep order despite the new freedoms.

"There was a disturbance out on the street," Girauld said in his quiet voice.

"If there was, I don't know anything about it," she replied.

"That makes me nervous," Girauld told her. "I should never know more than a field agent under my control."

"Bullshit." Falkenhayn said it in English because the American way of saying it sounded much more derisive. And she'd noted the small look of offense that entered Girauld's eyes when she used profanity.

The ambulance, its lights and Klaxon turned off, waddled through the crowd toward the street. The low conversations among the onlookers died as it passed by, then started anew as many people shook their heads and wandered away.

Falkenhayn walked back toward her midnight blue Mercedes, listening to the soft footfalls that identified Girauld behind her. She had learned to listen for his particular gait in the back streets of a dozen European cities over the past five years. Of the controls she'd had since making the switch from France's Groupe d'Intervention de la Gendarmerie Nationale to Direction Générale de Sécurité Extérieur, Girauld was sincerely her least favored.

Sometimes in the small hours of the morning, she wished for the body-aching preparation involved in GIGN's counterterrorist training. At least they were something she could turn off and on as necessary. The mind games she'd unwillingly embraced at DGSE knew no bounds.

"You always know more than your field agent," she said. "When you don't, as has happened in the past with us, that's when you get nervous."

"This disturbance involved an American," Girauld went on, ignoring her words. "He has been ID'ed as Jerome Pollux from New York City, but I believe it is an alias. I think he is connected to that other group holding court in East Berlin tonight. The Vopos pursuing him were unsuccessful in their hunt. Check with your American friends and see what you can find out about him."

Reaching her car, Falkenhayn unlocked the door and opened it. "If I find out anything, I'll let you know."

"Don't try to be clever, my dear. This mystery man might be the reason Doeker is dead. The Americans had evinced more interest in an East German economist than our government believed warranted. Find out. And soon."

She slid behind the wheel and started the engine, glancing up at Girauld. "As far as Doeker's assassination goes, perhaps I need only look to you, René. It wouldn't be beyond your logic to simply kill the man the Americans were interested in just to see what happened."

Without facial expression of any kind, Girauld turned and walked away.

Sliding the car into gear, she accelerated out to Unter den Linden and continued east. She picked up the mobile telephone and dialed as she drove. "It's Orchid," she said, using the code name the American CIA section chief had tagged her with when she'd arrived in East Germany.

"Shit," John Scott said in an agitated voice. "Where the hell have you been? I've tried calling you for the last ten minutes. Where are you?"

"Near Checkpoint Charlie." She disliked giving her location. Too many nightmares ended with her being tracked to her car then killed. In a way, though, it made sense. There was no other place she felt at ease except behind the wheel of a moving automobile.

"Good. Christ, I've had enough bad things happen tonight."

"What's wrong?"

"We had a safehouse on Lenin Allee, not far from you. I think someone's blown it. Three agents were there tonight waiting for a special-interest arrival. Only now I can't get through. The Vopos almost got my guy, and now they're covering the area looking for him. I need you to make a sweep by there and see if you can make anything of it." He gave her the address, mentioning the names of the Conradt family who lived there.

Even as Scott finished speaking, she saw the first of the parked Ladas. Her Mercedes made her stand out at once. "No. It's too risky."

"Hey," Scott said in a harsh tone, "risk is the name of the game tonight, babe. And there's plenty of it to go around. I need this guy found, damn quick, and I'm nominating you to find him. That's why you're getting paid all those big bucks. If you try weaseling out on me tonight, I promise you the French government will be tipped to your sellout before morning."

She didn't have to fake the anger in her voice. "What do you want me to do with this man if I find him?"

"Just hold on to him and get back to me." Scott broke the connection.

Falkenhayn put the phone away and made the turn onto Lenin Allee. She wondered if the safehouse problem was just an outgrowth of the Doeker execution or if it was the start of a brand-new chain of emergencies. She had no answers. Experience had taught her that on nights like tonight, anything was possible.

BOLAN BARRICADED the door with the wrought-iron bar, dropping it into the L-shaped slots on either side. Someone tugged on the concealed door as he searched the faceless body at the bottom of the stairway. He found a Cold Steel Tanto knife strapped to the left calf. The tugging on the door was repeated as he stripped the magazines from the useless pistols.

He found boxes of canning jars under the stairway. Choosing an empty bottle, he dropped in the bullets from the collected magazines, then filled the mouth with strips of newspapers.

Two voices, both speaking German, echoed inside the small room from above. Without warning, a line of bullet holes staggered through the hardwood door and whined from the concrete walls. The absence of the roar of autofire let him know the men were using silencers. Someone kicked at the door with enough force to splinter the wood, but it held.

Bolan unhooked the coal-oil lantern and splashed some of its contents into the bullet-filled canning jar as the crash of breaking dishes erupted from the kitchen. Above him was a small window set into the wall and covered by metal sheeting. From the structure of the room, he guessed the window opened onto an alley behind the apartments. Whoever had set up the trap would know about it, too.

More bullets bored through the door.

Unscrewing the base of the lantern, the Executioner threw the rest of its contents over the door, then lit a ball of wadded-up newspaper and tossed it into the center of the coal-oil stain. Flames whooshed up at once, leaking through the dozens of bullet holes and startling the gunners on the other side.

The warrior removed the metal sheeting from the window. The opening was set high in the wall, hardly more than sixteen inches high and a scarce shoulders'-breadth wide, but low to the ground. It led out into the narrow alley as Bolan had thought, but had unexpected defenses from a garbage bin chained to the wall only an arm's-reach away. After that, there was the safety of the shadows again. He fisted the Cold Steel Tanto grimly. And now he wasn't completely unarmed anymore.

With a shrill warning screech, the hinges holding the door pulled from the jamb. Another kick forced it inward, scattering flaming wood chips down the stairs.

Bolan lit the coal-oil-soaked newspaper filling the mouth of the jar, held it long enough to make sure it would stay burning, then rolled it outside.

The door burst open seconds later as the bullet-filled canning jar detonated and set off a string of ricochets.

Hauling himself through the narrow window as the bullets went off, Bolan scrambled to his feet behind the garbage bin. The waiting assassins, at least two of them, recovered from their initial shock and unleashed 3-round bursts from their weapons. Feeling the sheet-metal sides of the garbage bin shiver against his palms and knowing it couldn't provide sustained protection, the warrior ran.

The warrior used his hands to rebound off alley walls, caroming painfully from the ground as he failed to clear a stack of trash cans in his way. As he rolled to his feet and heard glass crunch under his tennis shoes, he checked for the combat knife in his back pocket. When he found it missing, he didn't waste time trying to find it.

Bolan heard shouts as more men closed in on his position. He ran toward Karl Marx Allee, hoping to get back to the museum area where the shadows would be more plentiful. Here, in the residential section, there would be too many people to hide from. Even now lights were coming on in different apartment windows, stripping the sheltering darkness away. And there were still the Vopos to consider. Whatever group was pursuing him now and had raided the safehouse, they had nothing to do with the East German police.

A pair of headlights stabbed into the alley, destroying the Executioner's night vision for the moment. He sped up without hesitation because there was nowhere else to go, meeting the driver head-on as the Lada's brakes locked.

Autofire raked the grillework of the Vopos' car as Bolan vaulted to the hood, showering sparks in his wake. He had a brief impression of the driver's side door opening as the Lada slammed into the fire escape. The impact ripped the structure from the building, then the warrior was on top of the car, leaping for the ground. He caught himself on all fours, knocking the wind from his lungs, as more bullets blew the glass from the stalled vehicle over his back and shoulders.

He kept moving, throwing himself forward like a sprinter coming off the blocks. He came out on the street and was spotted instantly. Vopos on foot called out for him to stop, waving pistols in the air. He didn't slow until he saw a trio of men break from the alley a block down, their weapons up and ready.

A midnight blue Mercedes rounded a corner onto the street in a fishtail of abused rubber. The passenger door opened as it caught up with him. There was a whiff of expensive perfume, and a woman's voice said, "Get in."

The words were in English, and Bolan didn't have a choice. The woman was an unknown, but he knew what waited before and behind him. She took off before he got settled in the passenger seat.

Bolan looked at the woman behind the wheel, getting a brief impression of blond beauty before his attention was focused on the pursuit taking shape behind them. The Mercedes jerked around the corner as the Ladas broke away from the curb.

He looked back at the woman, noticing the small automatic in her hand for the first time.

"You will make no sudden moves," she said, "or I will shoot you and leave your body for the Vopos."

2

"The Vopos might not have far to look for either of us," Bolan said grimly, nodding at the pair of Ladas swerving to block the street ahead of them. Light from the blue domes atop the vehicle splashed across the windshield just before it was cracked by a volley of shots.

The woman reacted like a professional driver, cutting the wheel to the left and taking the first open alley. More shots scattered sparks in their wake as the nose of the Mercedes smashed through a group of trash cans.

While she was engaged in steering, the Executioner reached across the seat and removed the small pistol from her grip. "Don't stop," he ordered, turning the gun toward her.

"I don't intend to. It's my ass on the line as much as it is yours."

Her words were in English, but the accent was bland and nonregional, like a television news anchor's. Bolan glanced at her again, noticing how well she was put together despite the dowdy attire. The clothes constituted an effort to camouflage herself, making him wonder briefly what else the woman had to hide.

"I wish I could believe that."

She checked the rearview mirror, then looked at him. "You can." She pulled the steering wheel hard right when the alley opened up on Lenin Allee again. "John Scott sent me to find out if you were even still alive."

Bolan recognized the name. The CIA section chief had been mentioned during the conversation with Brognola. Still, he was on enemy turf, pursued by the police and an unknown faction determined to shoot first and ask questions after the fact. If the meet had gone as scheduled, maybe he would have opted to stay with the regular game plan for a time—at least until the promised meet with Brognola.

Now, with everything evidently gone to hell, the Executioner figured on quarterbacking his own plays until a friendly he personally recognized dropped into the action with a better scheme. "Name-dropping doesn't cut any ice with me," he said in a graveyard voice. "I've seen people dead tonight whose names I still don't know."

He checked the pistol quickly, finding out it was a H&K Model P-7 K-3 that had been converted to fire .22 long-rifle cartridges. It was a professional assassin's caliber, favored by Mafia button men, as well as by CIA hardmen and Intelligence agents across the globe. It held a full clip. He fit the magazine back into the butt as another Lada materialized before them.

The woman started to cut the wheel again even though she had nowhere to go.

Bolan gripped the steering wheel with his free hand. The woman's eyes met his. "Ram it. It's our only chance." He snugged his seat belt as the team manning the Lada deployed into the street. He didn't think of returning fire. His own personal code, forged back in the earliest days of his war against the Mafia, kept him from firing on any policeman.

The woman muttered something that sounded like a prayer, the trailing words of it lost in the flat cracks of the pistols in the hands of the Vopos. Part of the Mercedes's windshield sagged inward as the rearview mirror vanished. Then all sound was lost in the confusion of the collision.

Metal rended, screaming like galvanized banshees ripped by carbon-bit talons, tearing free of both cars in great hunks and long strips. The greater weight of the Mercedes shoved it through as the two Vopos leaped for safety.

The seat belt wrung the air from Bolan's lungs but kept his face from the broken safety glass of the windshield. The Mercedes listed badly to the right as it came through the blockade. Out of control, the vehicle skidded across the street, narrowly missing two other cars. It came around facing the wrong way in the opposite lane.

An oncoming car jumped sideways, trying to avoid a collision only to lock its brakes and crunch into a BMW. Both vehicles spun helplessly, coming to a rest in front of the alley and effectively blocking pursuit. The tailing Lada came to a screeching halt only inches from the civilian cars.

Angry voices filled the night, silenced almost immediately by the rolling autofire that cut into both rear tires of the Mercedes.

"Who the hell are you?" the woman demanded as she pulled hard on the steering wheel.

"Ask Scott when you see him," Bolan advised, pointing toward another oncoming car.

The woman heeled their vehicle over as the other car honked stridently.

"If he's the one who set up this meet," Bolan said, glancing over his shoulder, "you can tell him for me that I've seen better."

"I will." She looked at him, fire in her gray eyes. "Now how about my gun?"

The warrior gave her a thin smile. "Uh-uh. I trust me not to point it in my direction. You're a question mark, lady, no matter how many names you drop."

A siren howled somewhere behind them as they raced for Berlin's Red Square.

"You're a fool, then. How can you expect to slip past the police without help? Your contact has been blown. I can help you."

"I can help myself," Bolan replied. "Pull over."

The siren sounded closer.

The warrior let himself out, sliding the H&K pistol into the back of his waistband. "Keep your hands on the steering wheel."

"You can't just leave me here."

"You're a big girl, remember? You were going to take care of me. This should make it even easier."

"What about my gun?"

"I'm betting it's not the only one you have," Bolan said. "That's why I want you to keep your hands where I can see them. And if you've got any sentimental attachments to the weapon, you'll be the first seasoned Intelligence agent I've seen that did."

Keeping his hand at his back with the pistol out of sight, the Executioner ran for the shelter of the shadows. He watched the woman, making sure she kept her hands where he could see them. Once he was inside the alley, he slowed to a trot, senses alive.

Being on the run, in enemy territory and cut off from immediate reinforcements, had become a way of life to him, and he moved with confidence. His primary objective was to contact Brognola to let him know he was intact so they could plan the next move. The big Fed's words and tone of voice had let him know the current situation was a hot one. The dead zone he had left behind underscored that.

A brief chatter of autofire out on the street let him know the hounds were closer than he'd thought. He allowed himself to wonder about the woman for a moment. It would have been too risky to try bringing her with him. There were already too many questions about the operation without dragging one of them along. He turned his attention to his own survival again as a shadow moved ahead of him.

FALKENHAYN FUELED a cold anger burning inside her as she watched the big man fade effortlessly into the night. The man was too confident, too much a part of the shadows around him to be a conventional CIA agent. He appeared quick and deadly, more than a match for any of Scott's people. The chill in his voice was something she was sure she would never forget. The knowledge started a new barrage of questions floating through her mind, reminding her of how far her covert relations with the French and the Americans had taken her into no-man's-land.

She slammed her palm against the steering wheel as she tried to pull away and the engine died. Smoke and oil fumes drained from the front of the Mercedes in a solid gray vapor. She tried the ignition again, listening to it grind for a moment before giving in to whatever damage had been done to it. The smell of hot water and the sound of liquid hissing and spatters against the pavement told her the radiator had been holed, as well.

The scream of the closing police vehicle filled the interior of the Mercedes.

She reached under the seat and came up with a H&K Model VP-70Z. It was larger and louder than the pistol that had been taken from her, and more awkward to her hands, but the time for quiet had passed. And the 18-round capacity available in 9 mm gave her more confidence. She chambered a round and flicked on the cock-and-lock safety before tucking the weapon into her purse.

As she slid out of the car, autofire ripped through the thin sheet metal of the roof and tore chunks of blue velour from the interior. Glass exploded from the windshield as new scars streaked the hood.

Falkenhayn dropped to the street, using the car as a shield, knowing at once from the angle of the bullets the shooter was firing from an elevated position. Opening her purse, she withdrew the H&K and crawled on her elbows and knees to the front of the Mercedes. The engine block served as additional bulletproofing.

Elbows burning from abrasions from the pavement, she scanned the tops of the nearby buildings, using her peripheral vision the way she'd been trained in GIGN.

A brief muzzle-flash scored the dark night at two o'clock.

She dived instinctively as the bullets cored through a remaining portion of the windshield and whined off the street surface. Huddled behind the Mercedes with the pistol in both hands, she watched as the Vopos' Lada came up the street, followed by at least two others in the distance. Cursing, she tried to wave the men off.

Instead, the Lada swung around sharply, skidding to block traffic as the two passengers disembarked with a show of handguns.

Autofire blazed from the top of the building, cutting one of the men down at once and sending the other spiraling away.

Realizing that her instincts had been correct about the sniper not being part of the Vopo force, she whirled back to face the shooter's position. Leveling the H&K in a target position that left her open to the gunner, she squeezed off three rapid shots, then ducked again.

Another burst of autofire made the hood of the luxury car shiver, then died away, leaving only hollow echoes in its wake.

Falkenhayn stripped the spare magazine from her purse, then raised the pistol to fire one-handed at her target. She squeezed off seven rounds, counting them off automatically the way she had been drilled to, spacing them across the gunner's position. The shooter didn't immediately respond.

She kicked off her shoes and raced toward the building, gathering up her skirt in her free hand after pocketing the extra clip. Bullets spanged off the curb as she threw herself into the alley. The smell of refuse clogged her nose when she took up a position next to the building. She glanced around the corner.

More blue lights of the Vopos swirled onto the street, flanking the downed policeman. Men spread out around the vehicles and returned fire.

Knowing the sniper's attention was divided, Falkenhayn shifted around the fire escape and went up the steps as quietly and quickly as she could. She was jeopardizing her mission by risking a confrontation with the sniper. But she'd never been good at walking away from a ballistic situation when she thought she might be able to save someone's life. Her GIGN bosses had put that in her file the day DGSE transferred her to their offices. Her superiors had held it against her, but they didn't get many women agents.

She placed the automatic on the first-floor railing while she tied a knot in her skirt to clear it from her legs. Satisfied with the skirt, she went on, reminding herself she had eight bullets left.

Clearing the third-floor landing without seeing anyone else, she changed magazines, shoving the unused one home while she pocketed the other. She gripped the gun loosely in both hands, forcing herself to relax and not give in to the impulse to tighten up. She couldn't make the questions go away, couldn't help wondering if the sniper was a rear guard for the big CIA agent. After all, the American had selected this spot to stop.

Blending with the shadows as much as she could, she topped the roof and clambered over the ledge as a vibration from below told her at least one of the Vopos had gotten the same idea she had. She crouched behind a grumbling ventilation unit, then peered around the corner.

The sniper was dressed in black, as the big American agent had been. His assault rifle had a matte black finish.

Aware of the time winding down around her, she moved to take the shooter out, wanting those precious few seconds before the Vopo got there. If the man was American, she needed to know it. Too much of her current mission was hinged on maybes and what-ifs.

She stepped around the ventilation unit, dropping the pistol into target acquisition as the shooter's head snapped around. The assault rifle tracked instantly, tearing black hunks of tar from the rooftop as it came around.

She pulled the trigger without hesitation. Moonlight glinted off the expended shell casings. Her breath was frozen in her lungs as she forced herself to continue squeezing the trigger as the man turned. She fired at the center of his face, not wanting to risk the possibility her target wore Kevlar body armor beneath the loose clothing.

There was a brief impression of the man's face going to pieces, then the body was hurled backward by the 9 mm parabellums.

Falkenhayn approached the body carefully, keeping the pistol trained on the man's head. Clinically detached, she saw all four of her rounds had been hits. Identifying the man from a photo was beyond the realm of possibility. After checking for a pulse at the man's throat and finding none, she knelt beside the corpse. She placed her weapon on the unmoving chest where she could get to it easily, then went through his pockets. Finding no ID and no personal items at all, she took up her pistol again and stood with her arms out as the Vopo came to the top of the stairs.

"You will stand where you are," the man ordered, holding out his weapon, "and you will stand very still or you will be dead."

"I understand." Falkenhayn stared directly into the man's face as he came over the ledge.

The Vopo walked forward carefully, both hands on his weapon. "Drop the gun and turn around. Face the ventilator and place your hands against it."

Falkenhayn put her pistol on the rooftop, then stepped away from it and put her hands on the vibrating unit. She watched the man with her peripheral vision. She'd answered none of the questions that plagued her, and had only succeeded in placing her life in the hands of the Vopos. Fear didn't touch her until she noticed the man's hands shaking.

He was young. He was afraid. He was inexperienced. His knuckles were white on the pistol he had pointed at her head.

Swallowing bile, Falkenhayn struggled to keep from flinching from the sudden threat she felt.

"I have her," the young Vopo shouted over the edge of the building. "It is safe to come up."

Not wanting the man to continue to stand behind her unobserved with his finger too tightly on the trigger, Falkenhayn caught him glancing down the smooth length of leg revealed by the tied-up skirt and spun toward him. She used a foot to knock the pistol away. The muzzle-flash when it went off was pointed toward the sky, sparking almost a foot long. Still in motion, she used the Y of her thumb and forefinger against the Vopo's exposed throat, keeping it just short of a killing blow.

As the policeman bent over, gagging helplessly while his lungs struggled to take in air, she lifted her knee into his crotch, cutting his legs from under him. He collapsed. She took the gun from him as he went down.

Breathing rapidly from her exertions and the emotional anticipation of the moment, Falkenhayn took the groaning man's cigarettes and lighter from his jacket pocket and lit up. The tobacco was East German and tasted terrible, but she didn't throw the cigarette away. Her hands shook almost as much as the policeman's had. But hers shook professionally. There was a difference, and she'd learned it well.

Untying her skirt, she let it drop to its full length, adjusting the stiletto sheathed on the inside of her left thigh. She looked down at the groaning policeman. "Never," she said, "*never* take your eyes off a prisoner's movements and allow your attention to be isolated in one area. Next time you might not be so lucky as to live."

More Vopos topped the fire escape. Their guns focused on Falkenhayn at once.

"Let me speak to the superior officer," Falkenhayn said in German.

A short, round man dressed in a gray trench coat stepped forward. "I am Sergeant Sabel of the Volkspolizei." He moved slowly, gazing down at the felled policeman. "My officer?"

"A few bruises, perhaps, Sergeant, but nothing has been permanently injured except his ego." Falkenhayn kept her voice matter-of-fact. She took a final hit from the cigarette, then dropped it to the rooftop and stepped back. "If you would assist me, please."

The Vopo captain crushed the cigarette butt out with his foot. "Who are you?"

"That doesn't matter," she said. "I have a phone number you need to call."

"And why do I need to call it?" The policeman's demeanor hardened. "You are my prisoner."

"The phone call," Falkenhayn said, "will keep you from being less than a sergeant by morning. But only if you hurry."

THE EXECUTIONER LIFTED the small pistol instinctively as autofire flared toward him. He dropped to the ground and rolled as 5.56 mm bullets tore into the alley. Checking his impulse to return fire, he continued rolling, getting to his feet as he dodged into another alley between apartments.

More movement wavered before him. He recognized the sheets and bits of clothing strung across the clothesline just in time to duck. The gunner behind him opened fire again.

Certain a policeman wouldn't take a chance on harming innocent people with uncontrolled fire, Bolan straightened and raised the pistol into target acquisition. He squeezed off two shots, not noticing any recoil at all as the hollow pops of the .22LR cartridges exploded.

The gunner fell backward, his free hand clawing at his face.

Bolan moved forward, intent on taking the assault rifle the other man had carried. The pistol he'd confiscated from the woman had only six rounds left.

Two more figures appeared at the mouth of the alley, autofire blazing from their weapons. The warrior thought it prudent to move, charging toward the next alley.

Shouts trailed him, marking his position. He heard the frantic buzz of walkie-talkies, brief snatches of hurried conversations. He couldn't understand all the words, but he recognized the tone—directions, orders, narrowing the flight path of the fugitive as blocks and counterblocks were put into place. He'd underestimated the numbers of the unknown group who'd killed the CIA tcam, had definitely underestimated the fervor they held for their objective.

He rounded a corner, running flat out, intending to lose himself in the mass of museums across the street. He never saw the man before him until there was no room to maneuver.

The gunner wore a long black duster, a black beret and boots with a shine that smacked of a military background. The man dropped into a crouch as he released his walkie-talkie and brought up the assault rifle.

Bolan launched himself into the air in a flying tackle. He felt the searing heat of the assault rifle's barrel against his cheek as the reports took his hearing away. Two hundred pounds of driving muscle fired by survival instinct gave the gunner no option. The man went down like a house before a hurricane.

The Executioner stayed with the man, levering the pistol barrel up against the underside of his opponent's chin and putting a pair of bullets through the soft flesh into the brain. With the barrel pressed against the flesh, the shots were muffled, almost invisible in the tapestry of gunfire coming from elsewhere. The man shivered, convulsed and died.

Getting to his feet, Bolan shoved the small pistol in his waistband and fisted the H&K 94 semiautomatic carbine. He clicked the magazine out, found six rounds left in the 15-round clip. Kneeling, he searched the dead man quickly, coming up with four more magazines.

Red smears across the fingers of one hand on the corpse caught his attention. He rubbed them with his palm and found they were dry. Images of the red-painted slogans in the CIA safehouse spilled into his mind. The man had no ID. Only a few crumpled West German notes and a handful of coins were in the pockets. The watch was stainless steel, constructed like a tool rather than a showpiece, and bore out Bolan's assumption of the man's military background.

Footsteps echoed behind him. He rammed a fresh magazine into the carbine and stood as two men wheeled around the corner. The first man never had a chance before a double-tap of 9 mm parabellums in his heart drove him back. The Executioner's third shot caught the second man in the forehead as he tried to fall back.

Bolan moved on, stopping at the mouth of the alley long enough to get his bearings. No one else appeared to be on the streets. He set his course for the museums and stayed within the shadows.

IT WAS ALMOST MIDNIGHT when Bolan made his backup connection at the American embassy. The last ninety minutes had been spent in a frantic cat-and-mouse chase through the darkness, but no one had been near him for most of that time.

He'd dropped the carbine in a trash bin several blocks back after he was certain he wouldn't need it anymore. The Vopos had stayed thick on the scene, trying to make sense of what had happened, as well as to tie up any loose ends. The woman had evidently found her own means of vanishing.

His contact at the embassy was a small, compact man who would have looked more at home working with an accounting firm than the State Department. He had no questions for Bolan when the two met in his car. He handed over "Mr. Belasko's" papers after ensuring they were in proper order. Hal Brognola's current phone number was also attached to a note inside the visa. It was a West Berlin exchange, but no address was given, letting the Executioner know the big Fed had found no secure ground of his own to swap Intel.

The State Department man looked at his watch. "The U-bahn's last run to West Berlin will be soon. It still stops at 1:30 a.m."

Bolan nodded and got underway, knowing he wouldn't find a phone to call Brognola until he got to West Germany. Freedom was still more prevalent in East Germany than phone lines.

The papers bearing the Michael Belasko name were given only cursory inspection at the station to the underground train. Once on board, he took a seat in the back against the wall and kept his eyes from the lights.

When the underground train roared through the darkness between the East Berlin and West Berlin stations, he wanted to have his night vision as operational as possible. He'd dumped the H&K .22 conversion in the men's room before approaching the train guards. Still, he wasn't empty-handed. A pair of shoestrings purchased from a vendor inside the station were in his back pocket. They looked harmless at first glance, until a trained eye spotted the hard knot in the center of their doubled length. A windpipe would last only a precious few seconds against it.

The train arrived at the station, and he zipped his jacket against the fresh chill of the wind. Taking the shoestrings from his pants pocket, he tucked it inside his jacket.

He used the second public telephone he came to, dismissing the first because it closed him in too much. The phone was answered on the third ring.

"Yeah," Harold Brognola's gruff voice said.

"It's me."

"You caught a hot one, Striker," the head Fed said. "How are you?"

"Mobile."

"Intact?"

"Yeah."

"The safehouse?"

Bolan didn't pull any punches. Brognola was someone who demanded the straight skinny on a given situation. The Executioner respected the man because Brognola gave as good as he got. "Blitzed."

"Personnel?"

"Never had a chance."

"Son of a bitch," Brognola said in a small voice. "Do you know who?"

"I was hoping you might be able to help me out on that score. You've got a number of players out here beating the bushes tonight. And a lot of them seemed to know about me."

"My fault, guy." Brognola sighed. "I was supposed to be working through channels on this one because it goes straight up to the Man himself."

"At this point I'm feeling more into independent programming. There's too many chances of getting canceled through public broadcasting."

"This can't be handled through touch-and-go," Brognola stated. "We need to meet."

"How do you want to do it?"

"I've got someone to bring you in."

"Why don't you name the place and I'll see you there?"

"Can't work this one that way, Striker. You'll understand why when you get here."

Bolan accepted that. Brognola knew how the warrior felt about having his movements restricted. For the Fed to admit it was necessary, the Executioner knew they were playing for high stakes. "Call it."

"Keep a low profile. Chances are the Belasko name could already be compromised on this one, too. We can set you up with something else later, but for now you've got to come in clean."

"Right."

"Do you know where Tiergarten is?"

"I've been there before."

"Fair enough. I've got a man waiting for you. His name's Kirchoff. August Kirchoff. He's with West

German Intelligence, but he's assigned to our current operation here. He'll know you. I've got another number for you in case something goes wrong.'' Brognola read it off.

Bolan memorized it without repeating it in case he was being observed. The auditory hissing in the connection told him the present exchange was being kicked back and rerouted through a telecommunications satellite. It would be Aaron Kurtzman's doing from Stony Man, he knew, but it told him more about the importance Brognola had assigned to the present operation. He broke the connection and moved off into the night.

3

Forty minutes later Bolan entered the Tiergarten from the east. According to a pamphlet in his map case, the Tiergarten was a 630-acre park. The night and the foliage around him provided plenty of coverage for a group that might have successfully tailed him. Most of the people walking the twisting side paths appeared to be lovers enjoying a late-evening stroll. Appearances could be deceiving. Someone had already fielded a female agent into the mix.

A man stepped into view ahead of the warrior. The guy was tall and slender, and his hands were tucked inside the pockets of a beige trench coat. He went hatless, his blond hair looking almost white under the flickering moonlight.

"Herr Belasko?" His voice was soft and pitched low, carrying as far as the Executioner but no farther.

Bolan continued on without saying anything. His hand was loose and ready around the knotted shoestrings inside his jacket pocket. He stopped three yards away from the man. Sweeping the area with his peripheral vision, he found nothing out of place. Still, a professional could have found a dozen places to hide. The only thing that had convinced the warrior to make the meet in the open and unarmed had been the tone in Brognola's voice.

"Come, come, my friend," the man said with an easy smile, "if you maintain your distance like this, we shall surely draw attention."

"I was told you'd have a word for me."

The man faced him again. "Actually I was told to have two of them for you. Pittsfield and Weatherbee."

Bolan nodded and moved forward. Both words were from his past, from a time shared by only a handful of warriors even within the Stony Man ranks. Pittsfield had been where the Executioner had dropped his sights on his first Mafia target. Al Weatherbee was the first cop to log on to the Bolan beat.

"I'm not in the best of moods about this arrangement, either," August Kirchoff groused. "I don't like being brought in off another assignment and ordered to walk down a blind alley to meet a man I can't vouchsafe." He smiled thinly. "After all, I only have your word you're who you say you are."

Bolan closed the distance but didn't drift within arm's reach of the agent. "It doesn't appear to be a night for choices."

"Walk with me," Kirchoff said. "I'd rather stay a moving target than to become a stationary one." He turned and walked deeper into the heart of the Tiergarten.

Following a half step behind and to the left so it would be awkward for the man to bring a pistol into play if he was right-handed, Bolan keyed into the night. Rosebushes, unadorned and skeletal in the uncertain light, ringed them. Their fragrance hung almost forgotten in the air. Tall trees jutted up to various heights as the old mixed in with the new.

"Beautiful, isn't it?" Kirchoff asked.

"Yes," Bolan replied. A light rain started to fall, misting against his face.

Kirchoff sidled in closer to the tree line and turned up the collar of his trench coat.

"They tell me it used to be even more so," the agent went on. "Back before the war. It was filled with roses and flowers, and the trees and shrubs were carefully manicured. The Berlin Zoo stayed busy with German families anxious for some form of amusement or diversion. Open-air concerts played there. My mother was a cellist in one group. Now, even with all the deutsche marks that have flowed into the city's coffers to replenish the glory that once was, it is but a pale shadow of itself. The seams still show." He glanced over his shoulder at Bolan. "The same way the seams still show between the East and the West even though the Wall no longer exists to separate us."

"A wound never truly goes away," Bolan said. "There are always scars left behind."

Kirchoff nodded. "Yes. You do know what I am talking about. So many of you American agents come over here with a belly full of national patriotism, ready to defend your God, country and flag. But most of you never realize Germany has been a part of history long before your country was even discovered."

A van drifted through the street, its tires hissing against the wet pavement. Bolan studied the dark windshield but could see nothing. A moment later it was gone around a bend, but the brake lights flared ruby against the bushes for a couple of heartbeats.

"It wasn't actually the bombing that destroyed the Tiergarten," Kirchoff went on. He took a side path leading away from the street.

Bolan knew the agent had noted the van's brake lights, as well.

"The shelling took its toll," Kirchoff said, "but it was the harsh winter that sent the Berliners into the Tiergarten to fell trees to warm their homes. And the rosebushes were uprooted to make way for potato beds. In spite of the need for beauty to quench an unforgettable thirst in a man's soul, he still needs to eat and stay warm and dry."

The German agent stepped up the pace. "I tell you this so you will know, Herr Belasko. The reunification of the Germanys is a lot like the reclamation of the Tiergarten to its former stateliness. It is a beautiful thing to behold, a hunger in the hearts of its peoples, but there still exists the need to survive."

He stepped off the path into the shelter of the brush. A matte black pistol formed an L-shaped black hole in his hand as he drew it from the trench coat. "Despite the promises made by your government and mine, I fear another such harsh winter is coming to sear the German heart." He glanced at the Executioner. "I only hope you do not serve as a harbinger of that winter."

Glancing back along the way they had come, Bolan saw two shadows gather in the night. Their footsteps echoed wetly against the damp concrete of the trails. Short-brimmed hats muted their features, but there was no disguising the snub-nosed automatic weapons gripped tightly in their hands.

Kirchoff crouched silently, the pistol held loosely between his ankles as his arms rested lightly on his knees. His eyes were keen and alert. "Did you get a look at them?" he whispered after the men had gone by.

Bolan shook his head.

"Neither did I." The agent sighed and remained stooped over as he threaded his way into thicker brush. "Who knows you're here?"

"Everything came to me through your channels."

"The CIA had its operation unmasked once tonight," Kirchoff said. "Otherwise your arrival in East Berlin would have gone through as planned."

"Maybe the chances of that happening were over when the BND learned of it," Bolan replied, hunkering beside the German agent.

Kirchoff parted the brush with a cautious hand. "My agency had nothing to do with what happened at the CIA safehouse. From field reports I was given access to only a few moments before your arrival here, it appears that some splinter group of the Red Army Faction penetrated the safehouse and killed the American agents."

"They also killed an elderly East German couple who were acting as custodians for the place."

"That's not uncommon for the RAF. They've been known to plant car bombs targeting West German businessmen working for United States companies."

A man's silhouette drifted into the opening on the other side of the underbrush and stopped by a large birdbath. Lightning flashed, dancing down the blued length of the barrel of the pistol he held.

"The problem we are faced with here," Kirchoff whispered as he released the brush and let the branches close together again, "is that the people following us might be comrades in arms instead of an enemy. There have been many layers of disinformation concerning your insertion here tonight. It's a most confusing problem we have set before us."

Bolan silently agreed as he watched the lean silhouette disappear back into the darkness.

SHIVERING UNDER the downpour of cold rain covering West Berlin, Firenze Falkenhayn darted from her newly acquired Volkswagen to the public phones on the other side of checkpoint Charlie. The 9 mm automatic weighed heavily in the pocket of her knee-length coat. She started dialing from memory, suddenly realized she wasn't sure exactly which number she had started punching in, then hung up and began again.

Girauld answered on the first ring. *"Oui?"*

Ignoring the man's use of French, Falkenhayn spoke German. Her feet were cold and wet, raw from the tangled stocking shreds. She felt exhausted, almost to the point of not caring if she was hunted or not. Her craving for a cigarette was intense, but she refused to give in to it because that brief, flickering moment would provide a sniper all the time he needed to target her. "Me," she said simply.

The Frenchman's voice shifted through layers of sleep at once. "I'd heard things at your end had gotten extremely hot. There were some people killed."

Unable to curb her anger and frustrated by his total lack of regard for her, Falkenhayn said, "I'm fine. Thanks for asking and being so concerned with my welfare."

"I knew you were all right or you wouldn't be making this call," Girauld countered in an unemotional tone. "Now put your personal feelings aside and give me the gist of it."

Falkenhayn took a deep breath and did so. She watched the traffic flowing from East to West and back again with interest, alert for anyone who might show too much interest in the little gray Volkswagen Beetle parked at the curb. She'd taken pains to acquire West Berlin plates, though, with the Wall down, East German plates were becoming commonplace.

"The CIA team members are all dead?" Girauld asked.

"Yes."

"You're sure of this?"

"Yes." Sergeant Sabel of the Volkspolizei had been very kind and considerate, and extremely informative after his phone call. She had gone into the safehouse herself to verify everything. The odor of death still left a bad taste in her mouth.

"What of the man they waited for?"

"He escaped." Falkenhayn knew that information would be common knowledge in Intelligence circles before morning.

"Do you know who he is?"

"No. He's an American, but he's not conventional CIA. This man moved extremely well and took advantage of the darkness more like a military person than an espionage agent."

"What does he look like?"

Falkenhayn repeated what she had observed, not surprised at all that the man had left such a lasting impression on her. She'd never before had her own gun taken from her or been so close to having her cover blown.

Girauld repeated the description, talking to himself as he made additions to the notes he was taking. "Even with this, he could be anybody," the Frenchman complained.

"Once you meet him," Falkenhayn said with conviction, "you'll know it's him."

"Did you learn anything of the nature of his mission from the Americans?"

"They're not talking to anybody at this point. They know they were burned by someone, but they're not sure who."

"Naturally, in that case, you are suspect."

"Naturally."

"I'd advise you to be careful around them, then. It wouldn't be above them to simply decide to blow your pretty little head off to whittle down the possibilities. The Americans aren't quite as neighborly as the British."

"I know. For the time being I plan to drop out of sight as far as the CIA is concerned."

"*Bon.*" Girauld cleared his throat.

Falkenhayn hated it when the man did that. It meant he thought he'd found an angle she hadn't considered in her planning.

"Did the American see you?"

"Yes." She released a pent-up breath, glad he had only thought of that.

"You might keep that in mind. The Americans wanted him slipped into this witch's brew quietly and unnoticed. He, and they, will know you can recognize him. The first time you see him, it could well be that your survival will depend on how quick you are with your gun."

"I'll keep that in mind."

"You do that. Maybe it will even save your life." His laugh was dry and mirthless.

Falkenhayn resisted the impulse to hang up. With the advent of the new CIA man, with her face known to one more faction of the Intelligence networks she was in frequent contact with, her problems had increased dramatically. She studied her pale reflection in the phone booth glass and brushed a strand of hair from her eyes.

"Did you learn anything more of Doeker or why he was assassinated?"

"No." She eased one foot out of her shoe and flexed her toes, almost sighing with satisfaction. Then she freed the other.

"I have." Girauld flipped pages in a notebook, and the sound mixed in with the crisp static on the connection. "His office was firebombed only moments after he is assumed to have been shot dead."

"That rules out the possibility that the assassin was working alone," Falkenhayn said.

"True. But if you assume the Americans were innocent of his death, and I'm not at this point, you have to also assume the assassin was not working alone because other members of his team were also busy attacking the CIA safehouse."

"You're describing a large force."

"Yes."

"And that means a native one."

Girauld sighed. "At this point our superiors believe so. But the question still remains whether it is East German or West German."

"There is always the Red Army Faction."

"We haven't ruled out that possibility, but my orders are to continue searching for an East German link."

"Despite the fact that part of the RAF has assassinated foreign Intelligence agents?"

"Yes. My team has been assigned to uncover links to the Russians. And that assignment includes you."

"Doesn't the home office know Russian Intelligence has been hit by the RAF, as well?"

"Yes, and it has been decided the Russians could easily engineer the deaths of some of their lesser agents to help them reach their goal of retaining control over East Germany's economic and political future."

"They truly think that's what's behind these assassinations?"

"I don't know. All I know for sure is that I have been given a job to do. And I mean to do it."

Gripping the phone tightly in her hand, Falkenhayn forced her voice to remain calm. "Aren't they aware of how hopeless it is for Russia to remain in control of East Germany? It is foolishness to believe the Russians would even try a subterfuge like this."

Girauld's voice hardened. "Wars have been fought for less, girl. You should keep that in mind. Your generation does not know of the terrors the German army performed not so long ago that have lived on in the minds of many people. They see a united Germany as a brand-new continent surfacing in Europe, filled with more threats than hopes. Germany has been birthed and raised on blood and steel, and there is no reason to believe that heritage will change now. That is one thing the French and Russian peoples have in common—the fear of the rebirth of the strongest enemy they have ever known. But it would not be seemly for the French government to be blamed in any way for this.''

"The time now is not like the time then," Falkenhayn protested. "You can't compare the two. Dozens of events have shaped the world since—''

Girauld interrupted her. "We both have jobs to do. I suggest we tend to them in the manner we have been trained for, rather than trying to second-guess the decisions of politicians." He broke the connection.

Falkenhayn controlled her anger with effort. She made herself exhale, then dropped coins into the machine and dialed the number she'd given the Vopo sergeant. It was picked up on the fourth ring.

"Yes?"

"This is becoming increasingly difficult," Falkenhayn said without preamble. She felt some of the tension drain away. Talking with Rudolph Perbandt was much different than talking with Girauld. With Perbandt there was always that feeling that she was working with a man who knew his place in the scheme of things rather than just as a cog in a wheel.

"Ah, Firenze, how are you?"

"Alive for the moment, though I'm beginning to feel even those are numbered."

"You're speaking of the incident at the CIA safehouse?"

"That's one of them."

"Rest assured that Sabel's orders have already been cut, transferring him to the Warsaw border. The men who saw you have been parceled off to different places, as well. So you should have plenty of room on both sides of the border to operate effectively."

"There is still the matter of the American. He saw me."

"I've already picked up his trail again. Even as we speak, Darmstader and his men are closing in on this mystery agent and his West German contact. If they can't bring them in, they have orders to kill them both."

"Relationships between the East and West will be even more strained if this comes out."

"Let me worry about that," Perbandt soothed. "No matter what happens, I will not have you compromised at this point. You are simply too valuable where you are."

Falkenhayn remained silent, refusing to give in to the desire to tell Perbandt that she wanted to be brought in after this assignment. Then she realized how optimistic she was being. She might not even live that long. She bit her lip in frustration.

"Firenze?"

"I'm here."

"And?"

"I'm thinking."

"About what?"

"Where Krispin Doeker fits into all of this."

"Maybe we'll never know."

From the sound of slight puffing on his end, Falkenhayn knew the man was stoking his pipe. For a moment she had a brief image of him in robe and slippers, perhaps even a nightcap. She dismissed the idea immediately. Despite his age and looks, Perbandt was one of the deadliest men she knew.

"Are you sure the French were not involved with Doeker's death?" Perbandt asked.

"Yes. They are just as concerned over his death as our government appears to be. What made an economist so important?"

"Having knowledge of that would do you no good where your assignment is concerned. Still, it is easy to see the dawn of this emerging new world beats with the power of the deutsche mark."

"And the dollar, the yen and the ruble, as well." Falkenhayn tried to keep the sarcasm from her voice but failed.

"Yes," Perbandt replied. "It is modern imperialism, stretching a country's influence past her borders through creative financing and ownership. Yet, as with politics, the end result sought is chiefly one of control." He sighed. "You've been told the next phase of your assignment?"

"Yes. The French are posting me in Munich as a secretary to a trade-relations representative trying to reach an agreement regarding the European Common Market."

"Of course. The French are aware, as is the rest of the world, that a united Germany can sow the seeds of a better economic future for those fortunate enough to get in on the ground floor."

Falkenhayn accepted what the man said as truth. World politics was a deadly game she tried hard to understand. But, as an associate had said—and a

Russian one at that—the closer you were to being a part of something, the less clearly you could see it. It was her personal conviction that the peoples of the world had a better understanding of the effects of global brinksmanship than the politicians did. After all, the people were the ones who had to live with the decisions.

"The man I killed tonight," she said warily, "was German."

"That doesn't mean he was an East German one," Perbandt replied. "You know as well as I do that East Germany is not being welcomed with the open arms that we all expected if the Wall was ever demolished. It is possible that this is some subterfuge engineered by an outside force to keep the two Germanys from reuniting."

"Which outside force?"

"At the moment I'm not at liberty to say."

Controlling her anger, Falkenhayn said, "So I am working in the dark?"

"It is the nature of your role in these matters, Firenze. You know that."

She said nothing. It seemed to her the past seven years of duplicity and loneliness had come to a head tonight. Everyone wanted her, wanted the information she could possibly offer, but no one was willing to trust her. The big American's flat refusal to trust her had summed up all the feelings her various controls tiptoed around.

"Firenze."

"I'm here."

"Call me from Munich when you get settled in. The timing could be crucial."

"I will."

Perbandt broke the connection.

Angry at herself for the resentment she felt, she hung up and gathered her wet shoes in one hand. The rain fell coldly against her as she walked to her car, but it was nothing when weighed against the congealed lump of fear in her stomach. She wished she knew how much good she was actually doing, wished she knew if her actions brought any good at all. The thing that terrified her most was that she killed and risked being killed only to bring about the continuation of the espionage game played between countries.

Hot tears mixed in with the cold rain running down her face.

KIRCHOFF LED and the Executioner followed, the rain helping to drown out whatever noise their passage through the brush might have made.

The warrior went to cover even before Kirchoff waved him to it. The same van he'd seen earlier coasted around a corner of a side street less than five yards away. The driver had left the headlights off, but blue gray smoke drifted from the exhaust system and the brake lights flared briefly as it slowed in passing. A hand-held spotlight flashed across the dark brush.

Bolan pressed into the tree beside him, feeling the rough bark bite into his cheek. The spotlight moved on slowly, leading the van. A moment later the shrill screech of metal against metal sounded as the panel door rolled open. Two men broke from the cover and entered the van.

The Executioner looked at Kirchoff. The West German agent held his weapon in both hands. He looked up at the Executioner.

"Stasi," Kirchoff whispered, referring to the East German espionage service.

Bolan nodded. The Stasi were dangerous men. They had been used to spy on other espionage agents within the German Democratic Republic, as well as the East German people themselves.

After the Wall had come down, a raid had been staged on Stasi headquarters by East German citizens who'd grown tired of living in fear of what the building represented. They hadn't found the torture chambers or political prisoners they'd expected, but the legacy of hate lived on. Even so, some East German officials had secretly culled what they considered to be the most loyal of the Stasi agents and still employed them to protect their own interests.

Kirchoff had been right in his assessment. The men hunting them could well be tomorrow's friends, but for tonight they had to be recognized as enemies. They were too heavily armed for a peaceful confrontation.

The warrior also knew they were there searching for him. Somehow he had been traced to the Tiergarten, or Brognola's inner circle was leaking secrets even worse than either of them thought.

Survival instincts flared to new life even before Bolan saw the first man. He dropped automatically, falling forward on his hands out of the line of fire. Bringing his left leg up, he kicked his attacker in the chest and knocked the man back into a tree. He rolled as another silencer-equipped weapon stuttered to a muted rumble and chewed up thick hunks of the black mud where he'd been a heartbeat earlier.

Scrambling to his feet, the Executioner scooped up a handful of mud and flung it into the shooter's eyes. The man was a professional. He kept the Uzi at waist level while he squeezed off 3- and 5-round bursts. Bolan went in low, like an attacking lineman breaking up a sweep play. His shoulder smashed against the gunner's knees and something snapped. The East German agent gave a bleat of pain before Bolan slugged him into unconsciousness with the captured Uzi.

The first man scrabbled in the brush, looking for his lost weapon.

"No," Bolan growled, drawing down on the man.

The man stopped, a look of resignation on his face. He held up his hands.

"Against the tree." The Executioner waved his free hand in case the man didn't understand English.

The man fell back.

Glancing around, the warrior saw Kirchoff getting to his feet. Another of the Stasi agents lay prone but breathing at his feet. A dark pool of blood gathered along Kirchoff's left side.

"You okay?"

"I'll live," Kirchoff replied. The hand holding the gun trembled slightly.

"Your man?"

"Alive."

Bolan nodded. "Cover me." He placed the Uzi on the ground and tied the man to the tree using the guy's own belt. A shirtsleeve, torn off under the man's jacket, made a gag. He figured the two downed men would keep until they were clear of the immediate area. He searched the one he'd dropped and came up with spare magazines to the Uzi.

Kirchoff took the lead again. "We had a nice plan to whisk you away from here tonight," he whispered in a pained voice. "Evidently it has gone all to hell. Those men back there belonged to Willy Darmstader. You can't hope to find a more dangerous man on the other side."

Bolan moved forward, slinging the Uzi as he reached for the BND agent.

Kirchoff's gun came up automatically, his eyes bright and hard.

"If we don't do something about that wound, you're going to bleed to death," Bolan told him.

Kirchoff lowered his gun.

Tearing the man's shirt clear of the wound, Bolan saw the bullet had gone in just above the left pelvic bone but hadn't exited. He hoped the man's insides hadn't been chewed up. The lack of complete penetration was a result of the subsonic rounds the Stasi agents had used.

Blood ran in rivulets as the rain fell against the wound. The pale skin of his abdomen showed blue black around the edges of the jagged puncture.

Bolan ripped a section of the agent's shirt to form a pressure bandage, then used the rest of it to bind the wound.

"*Verdamme,*" Kirchoff gasped as the shirt was pulled snug. He shrugged into his jacket when Bolan helped him. "Thanks."

"No problem."

"I've got a car out there," Kirchoff said. He dug in his pocket and came up with a single key on an unadorned ring. "It is not much in the way of escapes, but it will serve to get you to your next contact point. You will stand a better chance going for it alone. I would just slow you down."

"We'll make it out together. I made a promise to myself a long time ago to never walk into the brush with somebody I wasn't willing to carry out. Now let's do it." He looped the West German's arm across his shoulders and took some of the man's weight, then headed them toward the parking area.

4

"He's leaving the bar now."

Felix Scharnhorst pressed the minireceiver more tightly into his ear. "And the girl?" he said into the mouthpiece. His long body was cramped in the passenger seat of the Volkswagen sedan. He was made even more uncomfortable by the Heckler & Koch MP-5 SD-3 submachine gun tucked under his black duster.

"She's with him."

Scharnhorst studied the unimposing exterior of the eleven-story hotel on Landgrafenstrasse. He was impatient, burning with anger at the American agent's earlier escape in East Berlin. They remained unable to trace him, though Scharnhorst was personally convinced the man had made it safely to West Berlin, where his team was now. "Then she will have to die with him," he said in a flat voice. "Stay with him."

"Of course."

Scharnhorst turned to the two men in the car and nodded. They got out at once, and all three of them immediately headed in different directions.

Ignoring the rain that pelted him, Scharnhorst made for the front doors. The hotel was by no means cheap, but there was no doorman. He walked into the corridor easily, moving with athletic prowess that belied his size. With the black duster covering his six-foot-five frame, the folds of the material concealed the silenced submachine gun effortlessly.

He pressed the elevator button and waited. Seeing no one in the hall, he slid the microphone of the headset forward. "Klaus?"

"Third floor. No opposition. Continuing."

The elevator light flickered as it dropped.

"Elias?"

"He's going to his room."

Scharnhorst glanced at the hallway as an old couple approached. He was reminded of the couple at the CIA safehouse. The woman's screams and the begging pleas of her husband were something he could play over in his mind later. They would make the chill of the loneliness in his room seem much smaller than usual.

A smile touched his bloodless lips, causing an uncertain one to mirror on the old woman's face. She paused for a moment to let her husband catch up to her, pressing her hand back to take his. The old man's eyes blinked behind the rimless glasses, then quickly looked away.

The elevator chimed and the doors opened. Two middle-aged women got out.

Scharnhorst put a gloved hand over the elevator doors and nodded to the older couple.

The man started forward, but was checked by the woman when she stepped in front of him. "No, thank you."

Giving the woman a brief smile, Scharnhorst stepped into the cage. He smiled warmly at his distorted reflection in the polished stainless steel of the closed doors. The fear he could inspire in others was something he'd always treasured. He pulled the microphone forward. "Korb?"

"Fifth floor. There is no one on the fire escape."

"Let me know the instant any of you see anything wrong. These British agents are noted for their cold-blooded techniques under pressure. Madison has been in our country for a dozen years operating behind the scenes."

Three affirmatives crackled into his ear.

Satisfied, he tucked the microphone away as the cage slowed for the seventh floor. The doors opened and he stepped through, knowing Elias was positioned to warn him if anyone had been lying in wait.

Elias stepped from around the corner. He was a small man, with a lean, hard cut about him. A white scar marred his left cheek. Unlike the rest of the team, Elias was dressed in street clothes.

"Madison?" Scharnhorst asked.

"In his room."

"The girl?"

"There as well."

Scharnhorst led the way, Elias only a half step behind. "Who is she?"

"Someone the Briton picked up in the bar."

"Have you seen her there before?"

"No."

Scharnhorst glanced at the man. "Are you sure?"

Elias shrugged hesitantly, as if afraid to admit his inability to remember. "It is hard to say. I was there to watch the British agent."

"You watch someone primarily by watching those around him or her and seeing how they interact," Scharnhorst said. He hated working with unskilled help. Impatience chafed at him, his mind already involved in working out various angles of the situation.

The time frame they had been given to achieve a dozen different goals was staggering. But it could be done. With the money, the manpower and the political fervor he had standing behind him, it could be done twice over. The escape of the big American tonight had been only the first error, and would quickly be erased.

Scharnhorst came to a halt in front of Madison's door. He whispered into the microphone. "Korb?"

"Ready."

"Klaus?"

"Ready."

He glanced down the hall, making sure it was clear, then nodded Elias to the door.

The small man knelt quickly and slipped the lock.

They went in together. Scharnhorst knew the light from the hallway gave them away instantly. The H&K submachine gun came out from under the folds of the duster with his first tug. Elias faded from the line of fire.

Scharnhorst's eyes swept the room, coming to rest on the bed.

Jonas Madison lay on top of the woman under the sheets. Both appeared to be undressed and otherwise preoccupied. The British MI-6 man was short and stocky, with clipped silver gray hair and virtually no tan. The woman was well tanned and well endowed, with dark hair that fell to her shoulders.

Madison rolled away from the woman in a tangle of sheets as he dived for the Walther PPK/S in the shoulder holster on the nightstand.

Scharnhorst hadn't expected the silenced MAC-10 in the woman's hands that chewed .45-caliber holes in the sheets. He ducked, dodging a line of bullets that tore into the walls.

The woman followed him, sitting up in bed as she used both hands to track him.

Scharnhorst saw that Madison and the woman had been naked only from the waist up. The hotel room had been a trap to draw him out. He silently cursed Elias as he brought the submachine gun into target acquisition, a .45-caliber bullet grazing his Kevlar-covered ribs as he squeezed the trigger. He tracked the H&K across the woman's bare breasts on full-auto, knocking her back onto the bed and blowing the life from her.

He raised himself slowly, glancing toward the open window as Madison threw himself through in a surprisingly agile maneuver. Moving forward, the submachine gun canted from his elbow, he locked the microphone forward. "Klaus!"

"I'm here."

"Do you see him? He is on the fire escape." Scharnhorst looked back toward the door. Elias's corpse blocked the way. The woman hadn't been entirely unsuccessful in her attack.

"No."

"He is coming toward you."

"Yes. Yes, I see him now—"

The harsh bite of a heavy sniper rifle rattled in the street, scattering echoes.

Scharnhorst peered out, seeing the top of Madison's silver gray head. He pointed the H&K through the maze of iron bars and steps. A heavy-caliber round smashed into the window frame, tearing wooden splinters and Sheetrock dust free, and driving him to cover. He buried his head under his hands as more shots came through the wall. "Fritz!"

"I cannot find him," the new voice replied.

Scharnhorst scrambled across the carpeted floor. "He has got to be somewhere in the other building. Look for him on the higher floors. He would want a vantage point to do his sniping."

Scharnhorst brought himself to a sitting position beside the wrecked window. He used the 9 mm pistol from his shoulder holster to shoot out the lamp. Even with the room in darkness, he didn't try to move. Madison and the British team with him wouldn't try to take out their enemy without nightscopes. "Korb?"

"Here."

"What of Klaus?"

"Dead. I saw him fall."

"The sniper?"

"I do not know."

"Madison?"

"I am with him, but he will reach the street first."

"He must not get away."

"I am trying."

Scharnhorst got to his feet, then dived out the window. He crashed painfully against the metal grate of the fire escape. A bullet shook the frame, sparking in the night before spinning away. He remained on his back, hearing two thunderous reports go off above him.

"I got him!" Hans transmitted enthusiastically.

Regretting the circumstances that had him working with so many amateurs, Scharnhorst stood. For a moment he wondered if the British would post only one sniper. When no bullets pursued him, he knew he had his answer.

His boots rang against the metal steps. Madison was two floors below him, still racing down the fire escape. Korb was inside the building. Hans would only now be taking his leave of the hotel's roof. Neither of them would be in position to help him.

A grin stretched across his face. It came down to him and Madison, the hunter and the hunted. Exhilaration thrilled him. He ran faster, bruising himself as he bumped into the iron railings. Concentrating on each step before him, he knew the killing would take care of itself. It always did.

He heard the frenzied sound of Madison's bare feet slapping against the steps now, heard the groaning slip that cost the British agent a whole flight of stairs off his lead. He freed the sling on the submachine gun as he ran, leaving it hooked to the buttstock. As he made the next corner, he hung the strap to the railing and jumped over. Instead of trying to use the strap to take his weight, he let it guide his fall, dropping to the floor just above Madison.

Once his boots were on the railing, he hooked his fingers in the metal flesh of the fire escape and released the weapon. It dangled above him. He leaned down, aware of the three-story drop below, and grabbed Madison by the throat as the Briton came around.

Scharnhorst squeezed, then shoved. A bullet from the Walther whined off the metal steps beside him as he swung to the third-story landing. Madison tried to bring the weapon up again, but the German blocked the move with a forearm. A double-mule kick exploded against his midsection, bruising flesh under the bulletproof vest. He ignored the pain, concentrating on his opponent.

Levering an arm under Madison's, Scharnhorst spun the Briton in a wheel-throw, aiming him over the edge of the fire escape. A howl of surprise ripped through Madison's lips as he went over, his gun forgotten as he clawed for purchase. Scharnhorst drew his pistol and fired into the MI-6 agent's chest five times before the body hit the ground.

Scharnhorst took his time getting down despite the shrill scream of police sirens. He stood beside the dead man, gazing into the sightless eyes. Then he took the letter from his pocket and dropped it to the ground beside the corpse and walked away.

"HOW'S KIRCHOFF?" Bolan asked when Hal Brognola stepped into his room.

The big Fed unwrapped a cigar and tucked it into the corner of his mouth. Dark circles hung under the man's eyes, and an air of weariness clung to him. "He's going to make it."

Bolan stepped into a pair of dark slacks, pulled on an undershirt, dress shirt, socks, shoes and a sports coat. The Justice man had outfitted him with a Smith & Wesson .44 Magnum Model 29 with a four-inch barrel. He slipped it into a left-handed belt holster at the back of his waistband so he could reach it easily with his right hand. It wasn't the Beretta 93-R or the Desert Eagle, but he figured it beat the hell out of the knotted shoestrings he'd been carrying around. "What about the men we left behind?"

"Gone. No trace. I got a few tentative probes working on it, bouncing Darmstader's name around, but I don't have any high expectations. Everything about this operation is strictly hush-hush."

"I got that impression."

"Yeah, well, it might not get any better real soon," Brognola said sourly. "You ready?"

Bolan threw his towel back into the bathroom. "Shower, shave and a fresh change of clothes. Maybe you should tell me what I should be ready for."

"Who," Brognola corrected. He reached for the door and opened it. "I'll let this one be a surprise. It's likely to be the only pleasant one you get on this mission."

Bolan stepped through the door, then followed Brognola. His room was part of a rented suite in a West Berlin hotel that occupied the top floor. He'd noticed the heavy security at once.

Armament was in plain view. Automatic weapons, as well as surveillance equipment, were draped from the agents who manned the suite continually. A section chief paced the room, tilting his head as he waited for a response from whatever frequencies he monitored on his headset. The men kept their eyes focused on windows, black-and-white monitors showing a dozen different corridors of the hotel, and other pieces of equipment. One operative manned a portable radar station.

Brognola stopped in front of a door and knocked.

The voice that told them to come in was familiar.

The big Fed opened the door and waved Bolan in.

The Executioner recognized the man at the other end of the room at once. He entered and came to a parade-rest position before he realized it.

"I'll have to get back to you on that later," the President of the United States said into the phone. He clicked it off and set it aside. He glanced at Bolan and smiled tiredly. "At ease, soldier, we're all brass here."

"Yes, sir," Bolan said automatically, knowing the respect he gave came more from his military background than for his knowledge of the man before him. They'd met a few times before, on similar running-lights-off-in-the-dark missions as this one. From what he'd seen, the current President was a good man, willing to stay the course with his country and toe the line where the drug empires were concerned.

"I hear you've had a few problems tonight," the Man said.

"Yes, sir." Bolan heard the tiredness and anxiety trailing skeletal fingers through the President's words.

"Have you been briefed?"

"Not yet, Mr. President," Brognola said. "I figured maybe we'd take care of all of this at one time rather than parceling it out."

"Of course. I guess I'm thinking of those days with the CIA, of the way we used to spread the same story through layers of controls." He glanced at Bolan. "Can I get you something to drink?"

"Coffee."

"Hal?"

"The same."

The Man stepped behind the small desk, set out three ceramic mugs and filled them with coffee from a nearby urn.

Bolan liked the fact that the Man took care of his own personal needs without ringing for service. He passed up offers of sugar and cream, and accepted the proffered mug.

"First of all," the President said, "I want to thank you for coming on such short notice."

"No problem," Bolan replied. "I'm never called unless I'm needed."

"Still, I know that things are awkward for you with the way the situation is."

Bolan knew he referred to the arm's-length alliance the Executioner had with his government. But it seemed the only logical course after the destruction that had swept through the original Stony Man Farm. He remained silent, unable to either refute or recognize the statement of fact.

"It bothers me, as I'm sure it bothered the man who previously held this office, that you remain one of our country's staunchest defenders, yet we are unable to honor you for that."

"I do what I do because it's the only course I can follow," Bolan said. "You'll find men like me in branches of every service and in every law-enforcement field across the nation."

"I know, but I wanted you to know how I felt. Especially now."

"Yes, sir."

A discreet rap at the door drew the President's attention. "Come."

A man entered, handed over a sheet of paper and left.

The President read it quickly, then glanced up at Brognola. "The British just lost another team over here."

"Son of a bitch," Brognola said bitterly.

The President crumpled the note, took a lighter from his pocket and held it to the paper until it caught flame. He watched it burn, turning it in his fingers, then dropped it into a glass ashtray on the desk. When it was reduced to ashes, he turned back to Bolan. "You know of the problems facing East and West Germany?"

"I keep up on current politics."

"Yes. Let me recap it for you, though." He paused, as if assembling his thoughts. "The two Germanys are facing gigantic internal upheaval at this moment. Communism, at least as an economic force, has failed, leaving bitter husks of financially barren East European countries behind. Politically the Russians are trying to hang on to as much of a buffer zone as they can. As you have no doubt noticed, they're not having much luck with that. Satellite countries under their government are revolting. Violently. At the crux of this revolution is the question of the reunification of East and West Germany." A sad smile touched his lips. "You remember that old saw about being careful what you wish for?"

Bolan nodded.

"Well, that's come back to haunt the Germans in spades. Sometimes you discover what you thought you wanted isn't what you wanted at all. Now, with the Berlin Wall gone, the East and West Germans have discovered the specter of an emotional wall that's proving to be even more insurmountable than the physical one. Instead of being formed of concrete and barbed wire, patrolled by armed soldiers and attack dogs, they've discovered a thing formed of conflicting economics, politics and jealousies they've never known. They're confused and frightened, and looking for anyone to blame for their discomfort. One of these countries being blamed is the United States."

"The CIA safehouse attack is the outgrowth of that," Brognola said.

"However," the President continued, "we feel it goes much deeper than that. The Red Army Faction has always been anti-American. It's possible they're taking a stance against us."

"But how did they suddenly penetrate our security when they haven't been able to before?" Bolan asked.

The President nodded. "Exactly. And we're not the only ones. The Russians, British and French have all lost key espionage people in the last week. Jonas Madison, one of John Major's boys, was just found dead in an alley outside his hotel. Despite an attempt to trap the people who are assassinating the agents, Madison and his backup team were killed. A small armed force invaded the hotel and killed them in less than two minutes. An envelope was found on Madison's body, filled with more hateful invective against American agents on German soil." He took his glasses off and cleaned them. "We've been compromised in a lot of ways here. I don't need to tell you how critical the situation is."

"No. I've seen it firsthand." Bolan remembered the bodies of the German couple in the kitchen.

"The problem is," the Man went on, "we're set up to be made a perfect patsy in this. I've already stated, perhaps prematurely, my stance for a reunited Germany. But we haven't been able to reach any real agreements with the Russians. The West German government feels they should remain with NATO even after the reunification for military as well as economic protection. The Russians don't want to see that happen. So it can be construed that both countries are fighting over the bones of what could be a free and independent country."

"Is that what's happening?" Bolan asked.

The Man shook his head. "No, of course not." He waved it away. "True, we're concerned over the economic power Germany could possibly wield in the coming decades, but these countries aren't going to be at peace with themselves for years even after reunification. East German business is afraid that West German conglomerates, owned partially by American business interests, are going to gobble them up. Already rising unemployment is a major factor over there. The West German government is paying unemployment to East German citizens, but they aren't doing so without complaints of their own."

"Another spanner that's been thrown into the works, Striker," Brognola said, "is that some of the prominent East German and West German businessmen have been assassinated this past week, as well. Rumor has it the killings of foreign agents is just a retaliatory effort to avenge German deaths."

"I'd heard about that," Bolan commented. He sipped his coffee, letting the twisting truths of the problem fill his mind. "So where do I fit in?"

The President sat on the edge of the desk. "We'd hoped to put you onto a man named Krispin Doeker, who might have been able to shed some light on the current situation. Unfortunately, he, too, has been killed tonight."

"They found his body only minutes before the massacre at the safehouse," Brognola said.

"By the Brandenburger Tor?"

"Yeah. How'd you know?"

"I was by there when the Vopos were cordoning off the area. A border guard told me Doeker was an economist."

"Right," the President said. "He had information on something big brewing behind the East German business world. Now we can only guess at what it was."

"You don't think his death was related to the assassinations of the other businessmen?"

"Yes," Brognola replied, "but in a different way. Whatever's going on, Doeker was a player of sorts, not an observer."

"There's another man we feel is close to the situation," the President said. "Jeorg Karlsruhe is a prominent West German businessman based in Munich. He's been finessing certain business arrangements between the two countries, and he's been close to other international interests played close to the vest."

Bolan read between the lines, guessing that Karlsruhe had helped negotiate certain Agency problems from time to time, as well.

"He's going to be our contact on this operation," the Man said. "But he's to be a very loose contact. Karlsruhe has problems of his own, and I don't want to interfere with those. But we can use his influence to tuck you away so you can keep an eye on things." He paused. "The reunification of Germany could well be a very volatile thing. Like when the two halves of the Red Sea came crashing back together and destroyed everything in their path. We could get caught in the backwash of that. I don't hesitate to tell you what effects the paranoia gripping the German peoples has on the balance of world power. We're trying to end this century with peace and economic stability in spite of the Middle East situation. But if some kind of restraint isn't shown, if some kind of trust isn't salvaged from this, the future of the world might be altered by what we say and do here tonight. Somehow we've got to find the means to simply stay the course. At least until this is over."

"We're not going to be able to give you a lot of help, Striker," Brognola added. "I've got people standing by to react to Intel you're able to give us, but we've got to stay clean on this one. I can get you into Karlsruhe's entourage as a reporter, but that's all I can do at this point without overextending coverage. Once I get you in, you're on your own." He grimaced. "The straws don't come any shorter, guy."

"If it wasn't for the short straw," Bolan replied, "sometimes we'd get no straw at all."

"THE PROFIT MARGINS are beginning to drop off, Father. You need to start paying more attention to the mills instead of pursuing this wild junket around Germany."

Jeorg Karlsruhe listened to his eldest son sigh in exasperation when he realized he was being ignored. They sat in the rear seats of the elder Karlsruhe's private Mercedes limousine. He drank his coffee from a small cup and gazed at the Munich countryside, thinking Oktoberfest would be coming soon and how much he was looking forward to it. He had seen more than sixty of them come and go. As a child they had been moments wrapped in fantasy, dreams of excitement he could reach out and touch. Now they seemed to contain more wistfulness than anything else.

"Father? Are you listening to a word I'm saying?"

Karlsruhe turned to face his son. "Yes, Wilhelm, I hear you fine."

"And you have nothing to say?" Wilhelm sat on the seat amid his piles of papers with a lap-top computer balanced precariously across his knees. At his side was a portable phone that could grant him instant access to many parts of the financial world.

"I have plenty to say. However, you seem even less interested in my thoughts than you must think I am in yours."

Wilhelm adjusted his glasses and gazed at him owlishly. "Do you realize the risks you are taking with the family business?"

Karlsruhe permitted himself a small smile. "You mean the chances I am taking with your inheritance?" He finished his coffee and set it aside. He checked his wristwatch, glanced at the countryside and got his bearings. Isaak was perhaps the best driver he'd ever had, getting him to and fro neither too early nor too late.

"Father—"

"That is the real issue you are dancing so eloquently about, is it not?"

"No, that's not—"

Karlsruhe shook his head. "Never forget, Wilhelm, I raised you. I know what is inside your head. You will never have thoughts cross your mind that I did not put there."

Wilhelm looked away, his hands trembling on the keyboard.

"You are a good son," Karlsruhe said after a moment. "Perhaps you are the most loyal son I have in the three that have been born to me."

"I do not think you are being fair to the others. Arne has done very well for himself, and done pride to your name with his service in the military. And Raymond has a business of his own."

"Raymond's business is piddling," Karlsruhe said, "and Arne's position is cosmetic, involving no creativity at all on his part." He pointed a forefinger at Wilhelm. "That is where I fault you, Wilhelm. You fail to seek creativity. You see dollars and cents, figures jotted across those damn spreadsheets your computers spit out at your command. You have no sense of the iron nerve and guts it takes to put a venture together. You are a good manager, but you lack the soul of a businessman."

"And this thing you are trying to do, these reunification talks you so gladly donate your time to, this is good business?"

"Yes." Karlsruhe let his voice be emphatic. He glanced at the passing countryside again, noting by his change of balance that Isaak was taking the turnoff to his mansion now. He studied the iron gates in the distance as Isaak lifted a phone and spoke briefly into it. "I'm trying to build a future for this country, and that is good business."

"In the meantime, though, the steel mills suffer from a lack of a strong hand at the wheel."

"I could die tomorrow. Would it not be the same?"

Wilhelm dropped his gaze to the lap-top computer.

Karlsruhe waved the thought away. "I am not planning to do that, nor am I planning to continue to ignore the mills. Schedule a meeting with the plant managers for later this evening, and I will go over a plan of action. I assume you have developed one?"

"Yes."

"Good."

"If the managers would only listen to me," Wilhelm said, "I wouldn't have to bother you with this at all."

Karlsruhe gazed in open speculation at his son, wondering if a hint of territorial aggression lurked behind the apologetic words. He'd lived so long as a dog fighting to keep possession of a bone that grew larger and larger. Now, at a time when he had the biggest bone of all within his grasp, perhaps he was becoming a bit paranoid. He forced himself to relax.

Isaak pulled the limousine to a halt beside the gate house. Two security men stepped into position as the electronic defenses locked on to the car. Karlsruhe tripped the control of the electric window, and it lowered silently. The chill of the morning air was immediate, letting him know how much he'd had the driver turn up the heat. For a moment he was face-to-face with the fact that he was growing old, then he forced the thought away. He nodded to the guards, and they faded back into the gate house. The window slid back up.

Wilhelm tapped the computer keys restlessly, then hooked the phone to the modem. "There is a new member in the ranks of the journalists you are putting up at the family home."

"That is another source of contention for you, is it not?" Karlsruhe asked. "The money that I spend on the upkeep of the journalists?"

"It is an expenditure with no payoff."

"Wrong." Karlsruhe watched his son blink and recoil from his sudden bark. "It is a payoff you simply cannot measure with that dollars-and-cents yardstick you use. When you see what we are able to net, then you will see the amount you consider to be simply largesse to be payment well below what we receive."

"As you say, Father." Wilhelm folded up his papers, computer and modem, and prepared to debark as the limousine drew to a halt in front of the mansion.

Karlsruhe stepped out of the car first, gazing up at the three stories of stately manor house. He clasped his silver hawk-headed cane and walked toward the door, drawing his overcoat more tightly around him. "Who is the new man?"

Wilhelm maintained a slight distance behind his father. "His name is Michael McKay. He is a free-lance journalist working on assignment for one of the Washington papers."

"Good," Karlsruhe said, starting up the first of the stone steps, "another American. Their press is always most interesting. I will look forward to it. And, Wilhelm?"

"Yes, Father?"

He turned to look at his son as they entered the door, handing his hat and coat to his valet. "Keep in mind that reunification is the thing I hold most dear to my heart these days. The steel mills will survive. They always have. The German people may not." He turned and walked away before Wilhelm could reply.

5

"You will find Herr Karlsruhe to be a very generous host, Herr McKay," the chauffeur said into the rearview mirror. "However, don't expect the same kind of response from the younger Karlsruhe. Wilhelm is a penny-pincher, with the soul of a peasant."

Mack Bolan noted the security inside the spacious estate as they passed the gate house. He knew from the specs Brognola had provided that the huge garage east of the main house held a fleet of luxury automobiles, as well as an eight-man security team on the second floor. The helipad behind the Olympic-size pool in back held two helicopters with two more only minutes away. The pair held in reserve were equipped with chain guns, rocket launchers and modern surveillance systems.

Inside the walls infrared systems and motion detectors helped back up the human eyes Karlsruhe paid for. At night the foot patrols were enhanced by specially trained dogs.

"I'll keep that in mind," Bolan replied as they pulled to a stop in front of the main house. It was white, almost plain, rather than the ornate monster he'd expected. Over thirty rooms, Brognola's Intel had informed him. Small patios jutted from some of the upper bedrooms. A few men and women lounged around small white tables under colorful umbrellas. The warrior figured they represented some of the body of journalists Karlsruhe kept on hand to cover German reunification plans.

A pair of men in dark business suits hurried down the steps to meet the car as Bolan got out. They wore black gloves and sunglasses. Their hair was cut short, in military fashion, and their movements suggested the hairstyle wasn't just cosmetic.

"Remain by the car, please," the taller of the two men said in accented English. His coat gaped open enough to reveal the mini-Uzi holstered butt-forward over his left hip.

The other man moved forward, advancing cautiously.

Bolan dropped his duffel and put his hands on top of his head. A murmur of voices drew his attention upward.

Two men and three women had abandoned their patio table for the railing on the second floor to peer down at him in amusement. One of the women blew him a kiss and waved.

Bolan grinned back in response, already blending in with the group by herd instinct: just one of the guys sharing the misery.

"There is no need to place your hands on your head, Herr McKay," the guard said. "As long as you are who you say you are, there should be no problem and this will only be a formality."

Bolan exercised the McKay persona of a world-weary reporter, and cracked, "If I'd known this was going to be formal, I'd have dressed for it." He wore faded jeans, white tennis shoes with red-and-black racing stripes, a green polo shirt and gold-rimmed aviator sunglasses. "And you can call me Mike. I'm not really into formality." He dropped his hands to his sides as the other man finished frisking him, tossing Bolan's wallet to the first man.

The guard in charge went through the contents of the wallet while the other man opened the duffel.

Leaning back against the limousine, Bolan took a pack of cigarettes and a lighter from his jeans pocket. He lit up and closed the lighter with a flourish.

The guard stuck his hand out, indicating the lighter. "Please."

Bolan passed it over. "You boys have been watching too many James Bond films," he said with a grin.

"These are dangerous times," the guard replied, taking the lighter apart. Apparently he'd been satisfied with the McKay paperwork and visa. He handed lighter and wallet back at the same time.

"Nothing here," the other guard said, zipping up the duffel. "Clothing, toiletries and a lap-top computer."

"We will need to hang on to the computer for a time, Herr McKay," the guard in charge said. He gave a mirthless smile. "You would be surprised how much plastic explosives can be fit in around the frame."

"Yeah, well, technology's a wonderful thing, isn't it? You might want to check to see if it's wired up to a couple ICBMs while you're at it."

The smile flickered across the thin lips again. "Maybe we will at that. You Americans have a fondness for gadgets, as the Japanese have discovered."

Bolan laughed as he shouldered his duffel. The man was a professional with a tough job, and the warrior recognized that.

"If it comes up clean, you will get it back this evening."

"According to Herr Karlsruhe's agenda," the warrior said as he fell into step with the guards and returned to the house, "he has a speech today at noon."

"Yes."

"I may need my computer before then," Bolan said, playing up his role as a reporter. "How do you expect me to do my job without it?"

The guard smiled. "You will find pencils and a pad of paper in your room if you ask the staff. Surely you remember how to use those."

Once inside the house, the guards peeled back and went down a hallway off the foyer while Bolan was confronted by the butler. The man was officious and neat, but younger than he should have been to have arrived at his station of office through seniority. The Executioner figured some of the security people doubled as servants.

"I'll take your bag, Herr McKay."

Bolan gave it to the man, gazing around the two-storied opulence before him. A highly polished checkerboard floor of white and black set the stage for a winding staircase straight out of an Alfred Hitchcock movie. A chandelier hung over the center of the room with dozens of rainbows scattered around it from morning light coming in through the second-story windows. Paintings and tapestries adorned the walls. Vases sat on small, elegant tables.

"Herr Karlsruhe is expecting you," the butler said as he started down a hall. "Your room assignation has already been made. I will take you there later."

Bolan followed the man. Judging from the cut of the butler's coat, the man carried nothing short of a 9 mm pistol tucked against the small of his back. That said nothing for an ankle holster. Karlsruhe was a man who believed in security. But then, with the profile he was running in favor of reunification at a time when such people were turning up dead with frightening regularity, it was only fitting. And even that didn't mean it was going to be enough.

The butler paused and rapped on a heavy wooden door.

A voice told them to enter.

Karlsruhe's man opened the door and stood to one side as he announced Bolan. "Herr Michael McKay."

Karlsruhe stood near the fireplace of the den, stoking the burning logs with a poker. Pictures hung in frames around the walls, most of them in black and white. The theme was political, and Bolan could pick out past-American presidents and West German officials. Bookcases lined two of the three walls, somehow giving a cozy feeling to the room in spite of its immensity. The subdued lighting helped. The desk was seven feet of mahogany, holding only a phone, a desk calendar and a small collection of primarily black-and-white photographs of beautiful women.

"Welcome to my home, Herr McKay," Karlsruhe said. He jabbed at the logs again, sending ruby embers flying. He wore a dark suit that understated the thin angularity of his frame. His silver hair was neatly in place. Giving a small laugh, he said, "It seems I can never get warm enough in the fall and winter anymore.''

He hung the poker beside the fireplace. Above the mantelpiece was a bottle containing an old-fashioned sailing ship, and a Luger in a glass case. A bronze plate in the lower-left corner of the pistol case glinted in the wavering firelight but wasn't legible from Bolan's position. The smell of sandalwood and burgundy pipe tobacco lingered over the room.

''I appreciate you having me here on such short notice, Herr Karlsruhe,'' Bolan said. ''I hope you weren't too inconvenienced.''

''Please,'' Karlsruhe said, waving him to one of the overstuffed chairs before the desk, ''sit.''

Bolan did.

Karlsruhe sat in the swivel chair behind the desk. ''Can I get you something to drink?''

''I don't usually drink before noon,'' the warrior replied with a smile.

''But it has to be after noon somewhere in the world,'' Karlsruhe finished.

Bolan laughed, a good-old-boys' sound that he'd found could break down language barriers faster than anything else. ''Right.''

''A man after my own heart.''

The Executioner watched the bright alertness in the old man's eyes and wondered who was zooming who.

''What can I get you?''

''Dark beer would be fine.''

Karlsruhe raised his voice. ''Mayer?''

''At once, sir,'' a tinny voice called back from a hidden speaker.

"A security precaution," Karlsruhe said in explanation.

"I understand. I'd heard a number of your colleagues have already been injured or killed while pushing for the reunification issue."

"These are dangerous times. What do you know about the situation here? Your editor said you were deep in Liberia on a story when he finally reached you."

"I keep up with world events," Bolan replied. "I've had my eye on the Germanys since the Wall fell. I covered some of that."

"I read the articles in the portfolio your editor sent me," Karlsruhe said. "I like your style. Rather than clutter up a piece with extraneous detail, you stick to the heart of the matter."

"Thank you." Bolan knew Aaron Kurtzman kept the McKay cover current by placing articles and stories in magazines and newspapers. He'd read the McKay stories on Germany after the debriefing before the trip to Karlsruhe's Munich home. The writing *was* good.

A man carrying a tray with two glass mugs, two beer bottles and a shaker of salt entered the room and placed it on the desk. He left without a word.

Karlsruhe opened the bottles with an ornate opener from his desk. He sat a mug and an open bottle in front of Bolan. "To your health."

"And yours." Bolan poured, then salted the beer.

Karlsruhe took a deep draft, then wiped the foam from his lips with a napkin. "Germany is finally healing itself," he said. "After over forty years as a gaping wound for its people, the walls are coming down. Being able to be a part of that means much to me."

"I can empathize with that," Bolan replied. "Vietnam was the same for the United States. It played a big part in shaping my life."

"You were a war correspondent there, weren't you?"

"For a time."

"And you were a soldier, as well."

"Yes."

"I was a member of Hitler's Youth army, but I never saw battle until Germany was being overrun. Those are the days everyone seems predisposed to remember. They shudder in memory of the Führer's madness, and they forget most of those soldiers were only people fighting for a future, for hope for their children. European countries fear a united Germany. They say that every time the German people have gotten together, it's only been to attempt to take over the world." Karlsruhe laughed bitterly. "They fail to understand that again we're fighting for our future. Especially the future of East Germany. Even the East Germans have a hard time believing that."

He gazed at Bolan in open speculation. "And you, Herr McKay, what do you believe?"

Before Bolan could reply, someone rapped on the door.

"Ah," Karlsruhe said, uncrossing his legs and getting to his feet. He placed his mug on the desk. "It appears our other late guest has arrived." He straightened the lines of his suit.

The warrior stood, as well, reading into the older man's manner that the expected person was female.

The butler opened the door and announced, "Frü-lein Rachelle Moreau."

The woman was stunning. Blond hair fell in gently curling waves to her shoulders. She was tall, elegant in the simple yellow dress she'd worn for the meeting.

Karlsruhe took Moreau's hand to present her to Bolan. "Frülein Moreau, may I present Herr Michael McKay, of the American press." Karlsruhe stood behind her, beaming. "Früelin Moreau is with the French trade-relations group."

"A pleasure," Bolan said, reaching for her outstretched hand. Whatever else she was, she was also the woman who had taken him from the East German hellzone the previous night.

"WHO IS SHE?" Bolan asked, watching Rachelle Moreau talk animatedly with the men at her table. Occasionally her eyes swept across the banquet room, never quite connecting with Bolan's, but enough so that he was sure she was aware of him.

"Beats me," the *Rolling Stone* reporter, Rory Brentwood, said with a shrug, "but I intend to try to find out when this gig is over and the drinks start flowing." He was trim, long-haired, wearing a Brooks Brothers suit with no tie and dark sunglasses. In the street in front of the Munich hotel, the reporter had been mobbed by a group of excited youths. Karlsruhe's arrival had been a much quieter affair by comparison.

The banquet room was huge, filled with white-linen-covered tables holding maroon napkins tucked neatly in drinking glasses. Waiters and waitresses flowed through the room, freshening drinks and offering appetizers. Karlsruhe sat at the front of the room with the rest of the main event. Bolan recognized most of the men as leading financial proponents for, as well as against, the reunification of Germany. Some he'd seen for the first time during Brognola's final briefing. Others he had become aware of in the news.

"All I know," Brentwood said, "is that she has some heavy-duty connections with the French financial consultation team. She's like an up-scale secretary or something. I haven't seen her take a lot of notes on what's been going on, but she's been real interested in taking it all in."

Bolan nodded and moved away. He'd dressed to fit in with the crowd, wearing a dark suit, turtleneck and dress shoes. He went unarmed because no cover Brognola and Kurtzman could have conceived of would have put him close to the men in the room with a gun.

Doeker's death had raised the total of East German deaths by assassination to four. There had been three killed in West Germany, two of them in West Berlin. The only connection between the deaths, according to Brognola's Intel, was that all seven men had been pushing hard for reunification. Doeker had been a great loss. The economist was rumored to have had enough East German votes in his pocket to open the gate for West German businesses to begin merging with their counterparts on the other side.

Bolan tried to make it add up and couldn't. He was versed in the questions and in the problems, but couldn't figure the killings. But being on the inside looking out—as the Germans were—led directly back to the Americans and Russians, and perhaps the French, as well.

He accepted a coffee refill from one of the wandering waiters. His eye caught Rachelle Moreau's briefly as she turned around, then she looked away and Brentwood caught up to him.

"Hey, I didn't get your name while we were busy ogling the beauty over there."

"Mike McKay."

"Rory Brentwood. I'm with *Rolling Stone*."

"I know. I caught your act in front of the hotel."

The reporter grinned. "Yeah, well, I'm here to tell you even with all that the excitement's not what it used to be. If we'd had somebody here to interview Karlsruhe from MTV, guys like you and me would've never made it through the door."

"Would you gentlemen care to take your seats?" a waiter asked. "We are about to serve."

Bolan took a table at the back. Brentwood followed him. The Executioner stayed with the coffee while his companion took beer.

"You figuring on this gig being an all-nighter?" Brentwood asked.

Bolan guessed the man was referring to his choice of drinks. "Even when this breaks up, doesn't mean the news stops here."

"Yeah, well, it does for me." Brentwood spread his napkin in his lap. "I was sent over here to do a thumbnail sketch on this reunification thing, then do in-depth interviews with the German rock bands crossing over onto the American scene to find out what all this means to them." He smiled. "If anything. After all, music is music, and the masses would rather turn on a musician than a politician."

Moreau's blond head turned in Bolan's direction, but he couldn't see her face.

"Have you heard about those terrorist killings?" Brentwood asked. "The CIA guys who got blown away last night and those others?"

"Yeah."

"Makes you wonder how many agents everybody's got over here, doesn't it?"

"Not really."

Brentwood scooted back in his chair as a waiter placed a plate before him.

Conversation twisted quietly through the long room as the lights were dimmed and dining proceeded by candlelight. On the raised dais, where the main tables were, Karlsruhe chatted with the other business leaders.

"It also," Brentwood went on, "makes you wonder how it is espionage agents started dropping at roughly the same time the finance people did."

"Newton's Third Law," Bolan replied.

"What's that?"

"For every action there is an equal and opposite reaction."

"So two terrorist groups have set up shop? One to kill foreign agents and the other to kill Germans? That makes it sound like the Russians and CIA may be striking back in retaliation."

"The only Germans who've been killed so far have been people pushing for the reunification. Maybe you've got one group who's dead set against reunification."

"So what does that make the dead agents?"

"A smoke screen."

"Or icing on a double-cross," Brentwood suggested. "Say the CIA's opposing Russian intervention and under-the-table political pressure in the reunification talks, only they decide to take it into the streets. Naturally the KGB has to strike back. Pretty soon you've got a dirty little war being played out in the streets of two countries who are having problems of their own."

Bolan looked at the reporter. "Depends on how you look at it."

"I think I've got a hook to hang a story on." Brentwood raised his wineglass. "And until the truth comes out, a good hook is all you need to sell magazines."

The warrior didn't let the journalist's words touch him. He'd seen the good and evil reporters were capable of in Vietnam. One never existed without the other. Even the ones who'd covered the war right had let too much truth out to the American public without preparing the viewers. His first trip home from Vietnam, his mother had held him and cried against his chest, telling him she didn't understand how he could remain untouched by a war that sacrificed children. She'd spoken of the dead children she had seen on television, had seen in the magazines, then she'd looked into his eyes and seen the first of the scars across his heart.

"The way I hear it," Brentwood went on between bites, "these economic meetings carry more weight than the summit talks between Russia and America."

"That's because the Russians and Americans are trying to control the outcome of the reunification," Bolan said. "The spin rests on business, though, and there's not much anyone can do to the Germanys from outside."

"Except prevent them from merging. Gives a little more weight to my thoughts that America and Russia may be more deeply involved in the present subterfuge than anyone would like to think."

"You're getting pretty speculative for a reporter who's only here to find out what rock bands have to say about the world view, aren't you?"

The smile that fastened itself to Brentwood's lips wasn't genuine, and didn't completely cover the offense he took at the question. "Just because I ride in limousines and go first-class in this job doesn't mean I turn off my brain—"

The rest of Brentwood's rebuttal was lost as the sound of helicopter rotors filled the room, drowning out the background German folk music.

Bolan was in motion at once, pushing himself away from the table and yelling "Down!" He kicked the legs of Brentwood's chair when he saw the man wasn't moving, and sent the reporter sprawling.

Running lights of the pair of helicopters were visible for just a moment before kleig lights splashed against the large windows. Machine-gun fire chewed through the glass, scattering shards that spilled out over the attending audience. Screams punctuated the rolling thunder of the big .50-caliber weapons. Draperies were torn from curtain rods, then shot full of holes before they could drop to the floor.

A few of the security personnel returned fire, but it was ineffective. People were mown down. Two of the East German businessmen were taken out with head-shots, spilling blood across the white linen table-cloths.

The Executioner knew from the wounds that the men hadn't been victims of machine-gun fire. They had been killed with smaller bullets, perhaps 7.62 mm. He was equally sure the men using the snipers' weapons were in a stationary position and not aboard the helicopter.

He kept low to the ground, crawling to the side of a downed security man, pausing long enough to claim the MAC-10 the man carried and a fistful of extra magazines.

The warrior rolled toward the blasted windows, cradling the machine pistol in his arms, then came out of the roll in a crouch. The snout of the MAC-10 hovered a couple inches over the window frame as he squeezed the trigger. Brass glinted as it kicked out, spinning blackly against the ultrabright beams of the kleigs.

He swept the .45-caliber weapon back and forth, targeting the machine gunners, as well as the men handling the lights. The metal walls of the helicopter's interior kept the bullets dangerous instead of letting them punch harmlessly through.

Bolan dropped to the floor as the machine gunner swung toward his position. He duck-walked under the window, dropped the empty magazine and slid a fresh one home, coming up on the other side of the window. The kleig light had gone down under his first withering burst of fire. Depending on his peripheral vision, he tracked onto the Plexiglas bubble and the pilot's shadow. He squeezed off 5-round bursts, riding out the recoil, counting down six as he burned through the 30-round clip.

The helicopter wavered uncertainly, falling away from the building as Bolan reloaded. The second helicopter pulled back at once, trying to pin him with the light. Sniper fire—the warrior knew the difference by heart—chewed into the masonry as he focused on the big kleig. Brick splinters stung his face and hands, drawing blood as he squeezed the trigger.

The light winked out as something plucked at his jacket.

Bolan moved, reloading on the run, watching helplessly as the helicopters banked away from the hotel together. He gazed down at the street fourteen floors below.

Then the world slowed down again, and the full impact of the carnage surrounding him smashed across his psyche.

Security guards, bellowing orders in German, pointed their weapons at him.

Bolan held his hands away from his body, gripping the MAC-10 by its strap.

Before the men could move on him, Jeorg Karlsruhe stood behind the main table. He raised his voice, authority underscoring his words. The security guards fell back, but the weapon muzzles remained unwavering. Karlsruhe crossed the room, leaning heavily on the silver-tipped cane.

The warrior waited, standing in the shelter of the wall. The snipers had stopped firing, telling him either the teams had been rousted or they'd accomplished what they set out to do. Warning tingles buzzed at the back of his mind, just out of range of conscious thought.

Karlsruhe stopped in front of Bolan as hotel personnel carrying first-aid kits ran through the bullet-pocked doors. "It appears we owe you much tonight, Herr McKay," the German financier said, holding out a hand.

Bolan handed over the MAC-10. It was a face-saving gesture, but he got the impression Karlsruhe didn't completely trust him. More members of the hotel staff streamed into the room as anxious voices tried to quell the rampant fear.

Scanning for Rachelle Moreau, Bolan saw the woman on her knees, party dress stained with someone else's blood while she applied a tourniquet to a man's arm. She'd escaped injury. He couldn't help wondering if it had been by luck or by design.

He glanced back at the dead men at the table on the raised dais. There was no doubt in his mind that at least two of the predetermined targets had been taken out.

Karlsruhe passed the MAC-10 to a security guard, who slung it over his arm.

"Hey," Rory Brentwood said, his face ashen as he approached Bolan, "thanks for the save back there."

Bolan nodded, his attention drawn suddenly to another guard passing excitedly through the men and women across the banquet-room floor. The security man waved a walkie-talkie at Karlsruhe, speaking rapidly in German.

"Son of a bitch," Brentwood said quietly, fumbling for a cigarette.

Karlsruhe barked an order at the guard, silencing him immediately, then walked away with the man.

"What is it?"

"That guy," Brentwood replied, "just told Karlsruhe he picked up the transmissions between the helicopters. He said they spoke Russian."

Bolan caught Rachelle Moreau's eye, knowing the woman had understood, as well.

6

Outside the hotel Mack Bolan stood in the phone booth and watched the arrival of fire trucks and emergency vehicles. The private police of Munich, dressed all in black leather and carrying automatic weapons, fanned out from their cars. Orders, barked in frantic German, ricocheted from the street.

The receiver lifted at the other end, and Brognola's voice came over the line. "Yeah."

Bolan watched as paramedics streamed into the building. His own heart rate was still up from the footrace down the stairway. All he'd bought was a few seconds out from under official scrutiny and away from Karlsruhe's people. "You up to the latest in fast-breaking news?"

"We're tracking it now," the big Fed replied. "How're things at your end?"

"Messy."

"Our guy?"

"Still alive."

"That's something."

"Not when you stack it up against the other dead," Bolan replied grimly. Even as inured as he was to sudden death, the after-wash of it still clung to him with cold, fetid breath spilling down his spine.

"How're you?"

"Still in one piece."

"Your cover."

"Maybe. I had to take some reactive action up there to keep it from turning into a complete bloodbath."

A crunching sound echoed over the connection.

Bolan knew the man had taken an antacid tablet.

"It'll hold. The cover has a military history that goes with it."

"That's not the only problem. Somebody's got a player fielded at this end."

Brognola took a quiet breath. "You knew you weren't going to be the only one."

"Yeah. The problem is the lady can identify me as a player, too. She won't buy the cover."

"Who?"

"The name she's under is Rachelle Moreau. Could be her own. I don't know."

"She's part of the French delegation?"

"Yeah."

"Puts a new wrinkle in things."

"That's what I thought."

"Where do you know her from?"

"Last night."

"The woman who ID'ed herself as working with the CIA and later slipped through the East German roadblock?"

"That's the one."

"If she's covered, she's running a high profile."

"Not if they weren't counting on her bumping into me in East Berlin."

"If she's French, why's she doubling for the CIA?"

"Maybe she's not doubling at all. The Agency could have bought into an act. If she's operating on the fringe, they wouldn't trust her with eyes-only details anyway. But she'd get a larger view of her objective."

"The French might view Karlsruhe's attempt to guide German reunification as a threat," Brognola said. "What're the chances she was put inside as a Judas goat of some sort?"

"Figure them any way you want to," the warrior replied. "I won't bet against you."

"How hot do you think you are?"

"Hot enough."

"Do you want to scrub the mission?"

"No."

"Striker, this isn't supposed to be a suicide play."

"Yeah," Bolan agreed, "but I'm betting she's working under the same restrictions. If she was operating on the up-and-up, she'd have tagged me for Karlsruhe at the outset. The man's got his own private army at his beck and call."

"I know. She could have some of her teammates take you out when no one's looking."

"I'll be looking, and I won't make it easy. I've known about her for almost ten hours. If there was going to be a move made against me, it would've been made before now. I think the lady's got a few secrets of her own."

"Meaning she's hedging all bets to protect her own interests?"

"Yeah." Bolan shifted in the phone booth, watching as two of Karlsruhe's private force pointed him out to a trio of black-garbed policemen. They made for his position at once, hands resting lightly against the truncheons on their belts. "Has Aaron gotten any closer to ID'ing the hitters at the safehouse?"

"He's got a couple nibbles from sponging up the information circulating through the news satellites and BND private lines. Soon as I know something, you'll know it."

"Good enough." Bolan held the booth door, keeping the policemen outside for a moment. An angry face pressed against the glass, venting threats in thick German. "Got an even newer wrinkle for you if you haven't heard."

"Yeah?"

"Karlsruhe's security teams penetrated radio transmissions between the attack choppers."

"And?"

"According to them, the hitters spoke Russian during the strike."

"Damn. There's a shit-storm coming on this one, Striker."

"It's already here," Bolan said quietly. One of the policemen raked a thick-bladed combat knife through the phone cable, and the receiver went dead in his ear. He dropped it, letting it dangle at the end of its cord. Removing his hand from the door, he let them take him, felt the pain in his shoulder blades as they lifted his arms behind his back.

They asked him questions in German.

Bolan ignored them, studying the crowd gathered around the main entrance to the hotel. They put him in the back of a police car after handcuffing him. One of the officers guided his head in, then slammed the door. Through the streaked glass, he caught a glimpse of Rachelle Moreau. She turned away from him as soon as their eyes met. He settled into the seat as the police car powered away from the curb.

DAWN STREAKED THE SKY with rosy-tipped fingers before Bolan saw anything but the inside of a police station. The night had been filled with a series of endless questions. Some were in English. Some were in German. Some had to be translated both ways. The McKay cover held. He defied attempts to twist and turn his story into something that it wasn't. His mind had retreated comfortably into the sit-and-wait survival mechanism he'd learned in Vietnam. His interrogators were like men probing a black hole with a stick, afraid of what might rise up and strike. Surprisingly he was released before any effort from the American consulate could come through.

Now, on the outside of the police station, he waited with the collar of a borrowed jacket turned up to break the bitter chill blowing through the street. A pair of policemen waited with him. They sat in their car, sipping coffee and staying warm with a heater.

The warrior jammed his hands deeper into the jacket as the wind sank cold rat's teeth through the thin fabric of his slacks. His face hurt from the frigid intensity.

The opposition hadn't been idle during the night while he'd been sidelined. Snatches of news from radios and television in the squad room, gleaned from the American names and the pieces of German he knew, painted a dim picture. Munich authorities had rounded up recent known Russian and East German immigrants. No arrests had been made, but a sense of unrest was growing. Two more foreign agents had been found dead, a Frenchman and another Briton. Both had been victims of the same group that had destroyed the CIA safehouse. As before, slogans had been painted on the walls.

Bolan blinked sleep from his eyes as the long black Mercedes limousine glided to a halt in front of him. The driver got out and opened the rear door. "Karlsruhe?" Bolan asked as he eyed the driver.

"*Ja*, Herr McKay," the driver said. He wore polished livery and his boots shone. "Herr Karlsruhe only this morning discovered you were being held by the police. He gave orders that you be freed at once."

"I'll have to thank him."

"You will get the chance," the driver assured him. "I am to take you to him now."

"And if I don't want to go?"

The driver glanced meaningfully at the waiting policemen. "I do not think you would want to disappoint Herr Karlsruhe, sir."

Bolan gave the man a lopsided grin. "No, I don't guess I would." He crawled in the rear seat of the limo. As soon as the driver closed the door, the warrior tried the handle only to find it locked. Evidently Karlsruhe had already figured he might not be amenable to the invitation.

The driver seated himself behind the wheel. Bulletproof glass separated them.

The engine caught smoothly, and the luxury car pulled into the morning traffic.

BY THE TIME Bolan reached the helipad and the waiting helicopter, he felt warmed by the thermos of coffee he'd consumed during the trip. His combat senses were operational but quiet. The driver let him out of the limousine beside the copter.

"Herr Karlsruhe is waiting inside."

Bolan nodded. "Thanks for the coffee." He ducked and went under the whirling blades, feeling the cycling winds suck at the looseness of the open sleeves of the jacket. Squinting against the blowing sand and flying debris, he stepped into the open door.

Jeorg Karlsruhe sat in the back of the plush aircraft. He looked thin and dapper in the dark business suit. A white carnation decorated his lapel. His hands were folded in his lap before him. "Please," he said to Bolan, "sit."

The warrior sat beside the industrialist and belted in with a practiced hand. He took the miniature headset Karlsruhe offered and fit it onto his head. Immediately his ears filled with the rush of static on the air. The microthin speaker wire curled around his cheek to just below his lower lip.

The pilot and another man sat in front, leaving a row of seats vacant between them and Karlsruhe. The other passenger was a large, blocky man, made even more bulky by the Kevlar vest he obviously wore beneath his jacket. His hair was clipped, neat, military.

Something whispered at the back of Bolan's mind but quickly eluded his mental grasp. "I'm told I have you to thank for my freedom," he told the old man.

"It is nothing. I am only sorry I did not learn of your apprehension earlier. There were many things to take care of last night. Otherwise I would have noticed your absence before this morning." He gave a sharp order in German.

The helicopter pilot pulled on the yoke, and the bird's rotors cleaved the air. White-striped tarmac dropped away quickly beneath them.

Bolan watched it go, saw the long body of the limousine already rushing through the gates of the helipad. He glanced back at Karlsruhe, found the man regarding him with sharp vulture's eyes.

"If I had not taken it upon myself to see to your release," Karlsruhe said, "your embassy would have."

"If they'd noticed," Bolan replied smoothly. He wondered if the pilot and guard were monitoring their conversation.

"Eleven people died last night," Karlsruhe said, gazing out over the countryside. "More than twice that number were wounded." He glanced back at Bolan. "If you had not acted as you did, perhaps the losses would have been even greater. Whatever else you may claim to be, Herr McKay, you are also a soldier."

Bolan breathed easily, patient now because there was no other way to effectively seize the moment if that's what it came down to.

"It may interest you to know that I had you thoroughly checked out last night."

The warrior translated that to mean that Karlsruhe had known where he was after all, perhaps had even had a hand in putting him there until a decision was reached concerning reporter Mike McKay. "I'd assumed your people had already done that."

"They had. And I had personally counterchecked you, in light of your late arrival. I found nothing amiss then, and I find nothing now. The only unexplainable thing I find is your response in the banquet room."

Bolan let it lie. Whatever assumptions the industrialist cared to make were going to be the man's own. Bolan didn't intend to lead Karlsruhe through it.

"The American people tend to glamorize their fighting men," Karlsruhe said. "They think that every man who has enlisted comes out like Rambo. It is not so. For a man to become an excellent soldier, he must have fire in his guts and pride in his heart. He must actively strive to become the best, and in doing so he becomes a good soldier, as well as a leader of men. War is a crucible, Herr McKay, and the only men it turns out who have learned its trade well are men made of steel and blood."

Bolan knew that wasn't always true. Men didn't always fall in love with war and battle to become the best. His own career reflected that. He'd become the best because there was no other choice. Someone had to be the best, and he'd had everything it took to become that. There was a world of difference between a man who was a good shot and a man who would willingly take the life of another while hidden behind the cross hairs of a sniper scope. He could have told Karlsruhe that, but he didn't. The man had already formed his own beliefs. Americans weren't the only people to glamorize their warriors. German history was shot full of the same traits.

"I know you were in Vietnam."

"Yes."

"You were listed as Special Forces."

"Yes."

Karlsruhe studied him. "Even Special Forces doesn't explain your willingness to take up the fight last night."

Bolan said nothing. So far Karlsruhe's conjectures weren't boxing him in. There was still plenty of latitude to work with.

"Then," Karlsruhe continued, "I remembered Special Forces were often the hotbed of CIA intrigues. They headed up such projects as the Phoenix people."

"Yes."

"You can understand, of course, why I suddenly wanted to know if you were still affiliated with that group."

"And you couldn't verify it either way."

Karlsruhe smiled. "You are a blunt man, Herr McKay."

"Sometimes it pays to be that way in my business." Bolan kept his face neutral. However it played, the industrialist needed to feel no pressure from him.

"It doesn't in mine." Karlsruhe rested both hands on the silver hawk's head of his cane. "Usually. With you, however, I find I can act no other way. In business I can make people wait. I can use time to my advantage. People come to deal with me. I don't go to them to deal."

He pointed with the tip of his cane, indicating the steel foundry coming up beneath the helicopter. Galvanized sheet metal on some of the outbuildings gleamed in the morning light. "There. See it?"

"Yes."

"My father started this foundry. He supplied steel to build the ships in the Kaiser's great navy." He paused as the helicopter circled the area. "My roots are here." He tapped the cane to emphasize his words. "The German blood runs thick and healthy in my veins, and I have learned to be very jealous at my age."

Bolan looked at him, waiting.

"There is a new world awaiting Germany's stamp on it. I want to live to see it. I want my foundry to supply the steel sinews this country will need to become strong again." He smiled. "Perhaps it is a vanity. My father talked of empires, of the return of a new and better *reich*. For myself, I only want to see a return to greatness for this country."

Bolan watched as Karlsruhe spoke more German and the helicopter veered off. The green-leafed sea moved once more beneath them.

"Only now, instead of being my ally, time is moving against me." Karlsruhe looked at him. "But I am not a man who bends easily. Still, it is forcing me to make decisions on the spur of the moment, rather than questioning every forseeable possibility. You represent a number of possibilities yourself, Herr McKay."

"If you were unsure of me, then what am I doing here?"

"Because I choose to believe that no matter who you truly are or who you truly serve, your cause is the same as mine."

"I'm not here to unify Germany," Bolan said, relaxing back in his harness.

"That's not the cause I serve, either," Karlsruhe said. "I do what I do to bring peace to these countries. The Soviet pullout has left a vacuum in East Germany, as it has in all of Eastern Europe. But the pull is felt most strongly here."

"The people of Lithuania or Romania might disagree with you."

"Let them." Karlsruhe stamped his cane impatiently. "No other country under Communist control will have the problems left facing the two Germanys. We are two factions of the same people, left adrift by politics and economics. We must bridge those gaps somehow."

"Even if bridging them means bloodshed?"

"No." Spots of color touched Karlsruhe's cheeks. "There will be no German blood spilled by German hands to bring the two countries together."

"I think there already has been," Bolan said.

"You are wrong."

"You believe the Russians attacked the banquet last night?"

"That's what I was told."

"What about the two East German representatives who were killed at your table?"

"What about them?"

"Snipers killed them." The empty static rushed to fill the void after Bolan's words.

"How did you know that? That information has not been released."

"I saw the bodies. I know what to look for."

Karlsruhe looked away.

"How were those men positioned on a quick reunification?"

Karlsruhe's thin lips barely moved as he spoke. "They were against it."

"Why would the Russians kill people who were helping them retain some control over East Germany?"

"I don't know. I've been asking myself that all night." Karlsruhe looked at him. "The only thing I have been able to fasten on is that espionage games between the so-called superpowers have been played in my country for more than forty years. This could be but one more in a very long list."

"An economic division once threatened to split my country," Bolan said. "It made a lot of people do unbelievable things to each other in the name of liberty."

"You're referring to your President Lincoln's battles in the middle of the nineteenth century."

"Right. The Civil War."

"We learned it as the War Between the States."

"Could be you're in the middle of your own war between the Germanys and don't know it," Bolan said. "It would explain why espionage agents are being killed, and it would explain why German businessmen are turning up dead. Both sets of people represent indicators on what's going on behind the scenes."

"I will give it thought. My first impulse is to want to believe some outside agency is responsible for our current problems. Perhaps I am being blinded by my own hopes."

The helicopter dropped, homing in on the helipad behind the Karlsruhe mansion.

"Either way," the industrialist said, "I want men around me who I can depend on." He glanced at Bolan. "I have decided you are one of those, whether you ultimately turn out to be an American spy or a learned journalist with an intimate knowledge of firearms."

He reached under his seat just before the skids touched down and handed Bolan an oiled wooden box. "My gift to you, in appreciation for what you did last night, and in the event that you are needed again."

Bolan lifted the box's lid. Inside, nestled on a cut-out pad of foam rubber, was a stainless-steel Smith & Wesson Model 645 automatic.

CARRYING THE WOODEN BOX under his arm, Bolan climbed the stairs to his room. Karlsruhe had left him on the helipad after telling him the mansion staff had received instructions that he was to be permitted to carry the weapon on his person. The industrialist also informed him that .45-caliber cartridges had been left in his room. Most of the other reporters had to have been busy working on notes or extended versions of the previous night's story because only a few of them were around.

The door to his room opened at his touch. Long streamers of golden sunlight showered the room. The decor had been done in white, offset by light-colored woods. The bed was made. The draperies covering the patio were pulled to the sides. The extra chair was empty. His lap-top computer was open on the bureau, the 3.5-inch floppy disks scattered beside it while the liquid-crystal monitor cycled through another directory reading. His bags were in the middle of the floor with his clothing spread out beside them.

Rachelle Moreau looked up at him as he filled the door. She wore no makeup, but her face was pale and covered with a natural beauty few women were graced with. Her body was lean and slender, sheathed in black jeans and a flannel shirt with the sleeves rolled up. On her knees in front of her latest suitcase, there was no way she could deny what she'd been doing. A cigarette dangled from the corner of her mouth.

Bolan closed the door as he entered the room and tossed the gun box to the bed.

She regarded him coolly, taking the cigarette from her mouth to flick ashes into a disposable plastic cup beside her.

"I wasn't expecting maid service," Bolan said as he crossed his arms and leaned against the door.

"And I wasn't expecting you back so soon." She got to her feet easily, dusting off the seat of her jeans, then bending to retrieve the disposable cup of ashes and cigarette butts.

"I had some help."

"Your government?"

"No. Karlsruhe."

"Ah." She nodded, as if the answer explained a great deal. She glanced at the gun box and cocked an inquisitive eyebrow.

"A present," Bolan replied.

"From Herr Karlsruhe?"

"Yes."

"You make friends quickly."

"Apparently I make enemies just as quickly."

She gave him a slight smile. "Some men are born with a talent for these things."

"The problem is, I haven't figured out where you fit in."

"A woman's mystery always remains her final ace."

"Playing games can get you killed at this point."

She looked at him. "Rest assured, I'm playing no games here."

"Are you still here to rescue me?"

Taking a final drag off her cigarette, she dropped the butt into the cup and walked toward him. "No. You missed out on your opportunity for that. Please let me by."

Bolan stepped aside and opened the door.

She went through without a backward glance. "Take care of yourself, Mr. McKay. You're something of a mystery yourself."

He watched her go, calm and cool as her hips swayed gently from side to side. When she disappeared down the stairs and around the corner, he closed the door and locked it. Habit made him seek out the shells and load the .45. He found a shoulder rig with the bullets but disregarded it. If Karlsruhe's people knew of his armament and were going to be watching him, it would serve him better to carry it where they wouldn't be expecting it.

He put his things away as years of living in a military mode demanded. When his clothing was once more neat and orderly and the lap-top had been shut down, he stripped and took a quick shower.

Feeling clean but not refreshed, he pulled on a pair of gray gym shorts, laid down on the bed, stuck the .45 under his pillow and willed himself to sleep. His thoughts were filled with the jungle, then blackness swallowed him, leaving consciousness just below the surface.

BOLAN GRABBED THE PHONE on the first ring, dragged it to his ear as he sat up on the bed. Dusk had gathered outside his window.

"McKay?"

"Yeah." The voice belonged to Aaron Kurtzman, Stony Man's computer expert.

"You need to call me."

The warrior hung up on empty air and got dressed, snugging the heavy Smith in the back of his jeans.

"THE BND MADE ONE of the guys at the safehouse hit," Kurtzman said, "but they're sitting on the information till the chancellor's office decides what to do with it. However they put it out on the street, it's going to start a scramble between world powers."

Bolan huddled inside the phone booth in front of a small grocery store on a dark Munich side street. "I'm listening."

"I tripped over the guy's name while tagging along some of the avenues of investigation the BND computer boys were flashing through Interpol channels. Took me a few hours to run it to ground." Kurtzman sounded tired, as if he'd made every electronic mile himself.

Despite the precaution of calling the special Stony Man number from a public booth, Bolan watched the traffic flow carefully. Even if a spotter had been able to scan him punching the overseas number in, the call would be untraceable. The next time the same number was used, it would be rerouted to Nashville, Indiana, or any of a dozen other places Kurtzman had set up. Nothing ever made it back to the Farm without prior approval from the Bear. Even the numbers Brognola had for contact with Stony Man were different from the set Bolan had been given.

"The BND ID'ed him from fingerprints at the scene. His name's Norbert Meineck, and he's got a long history with the RAF. Definitely a nasty individual here. He's suspected of bombings, shootings and all kinds of vileness. If the West Germans catch him, they're going to put him so far under they'll have to pipe sunlight to him."

"The hit was sanctioned by the RAF?" Bolan asked.

"Didn't say that, Striker. The telltales the BND's hanging on to are vague about who actually put it together."

"Where can I find Meineck?"

"I got a list. It's the best I could do."

"That's all I'm asking for, Bear." Bolan knew from experience that Kurtzman's best—even when the computer systems man cautioned against his own Intel—was leagues ahead of the nearest competition.

Kurtzman read off a list of names and addresses.

Bolan copied them down, logging them in the symbolic code he used in his current war book when the chances of the documents falling into unfriendly hands existed. The symbols were drawn from his own past and experiences, taken in a shorthand that would make breaking the code even harder. He closed the book and tucked it away inside his jacket. The Volkswagen he'd drawn from Karlsruhe's garage fleet for the jaunt into town gleamed sleekly in the darkness.

"I got a lead on your mystery lady, too," Kurtzman said. "Her real name is Firenze Falkenhayn. She's French, a covert operator for the DGSE. According to the files I was able to leverage from the French, she's recently transferred in from the GIGN."

"That's the counterterrorist arm."

"Yeah. Seems the DGSE took her from GIGN after the German issue exploded onto the political scene. She's been a lot of people in Germany, East and West, over the past year or so."

"The French are using her to double against the Germans?"

"Maybe. She speaks the language like a native. Her father was East German. That's where the surname comes in. Her mother was French. I also accessed the CIA files when I cross-referenced her. Scott, the CIA guy whose operation was supposed to get you in close to Doeker, is convinced he's bought her out."

"Strange how someone involved in antiterrorist work would set herself up to sell out the minute she hit the bricks."

"Beats me. All I've got is the paperwork, and it looks good from this end. Scott's been paying her off right along, and she's taken care of some minor stuff for our side."

"But nothing that would compromise her with the French?"

"Right."

"It doesn't scan."

"It's your call, big guy. You've seen her in the flesh. Personally, if I was in your shoes, I'd be having second thoughts about trusting anybody on the other side of my own skin."

"If you have second thoughts in this game," Bolan said, "you're thinking too long."

"I read you."

"I need a care package."

"Hard or soft?"

"Hard."

"Give me twenty minutes. Anything else?"

"Get a message to Hal for me."

"Okay."

"Tell him to be expecting some flak tonight. I'm going to rattle some cages and see what falls out before morning. Karlsruhe and the other people heading up the reunification talks are sitting ducks if whoever is gunning for them is going to start playing hardball."

"Be careful out there," Kurtzman cautioned. "From appearances you've got one team targeting foreign agents in-country, and another dropping German reunification people. If you don't step lively, you're going to get caught in the crunch."

"I don't think we're dealing with two teams," Bolan said. "Once you get out in the jungle, you get a feel for the predators. Right now I'm only reading one spoor. I just haven't figured out what the stakes are." Bolan broke the connection.

He left Karlsruhe's vehicle where it was and walked, feeling better now that he had a way to deal himself into the action. Thoughts of the dead left at last night's banquet plummeted through his mind. There was no way to defend against carnage of that sort except to carry a cleansing fire back to the source. And he intended to throw gasoline on the flames once he got it that far.

7

Coming in from the Isar River, Mack Bolan stayed within the shadows as he closed on his target. The wind blew chill, chafing at his exposed skin not protected by the blacksuit. In addition to the night clothing, Kurtzman's package had consisted of a silenced MAC-10, an Israeli Desert Eagle in shoulder rigging, various garrotes, knives and a small selection of incendiaries. He hadn't been able to get his regular gear through channels in time, but there was no problem with the availability of armament once he'd arrived. Kurtzman's computers held detailed stashes made by several different countries.

Winter grass whispered across his booted ankles as he double-timed it to the closed-down warehouse. According to the Bear's files, the warehouse had once served the industrial freight trekking down the Isar River, but had slowly given way as newer and better train lines were relaid after the war. Instead of being torn down, it had housed a number of different family enterprises that had also given way to the rebirth of the Germany economy. Now it was barren except for the Red Army Faction members who'd chosen it as a sometime meeting place.

Wearing combat cosmetics, the warrior was nearly invisible against the warehouse. Gray-fogged glass panes set in long, narrow windows afforded Bolan a grim view of the empty warehouse. He kept his shoulders near the wall as he slid toward the slightly open double doors. Holding the MAC-10 by his ear, he reached forward with one hand and tugged on the door. The hinges were well oiled, and it swung open quietly. A dim slash of silvery moonlight fell on the scarred wooden floor.

He went in, holding the machine pistol in both hands before him. The door closed at his touch. He waited, breathing quietly, pausing to let his night vision adjust.

Kurtzman's inquiry had revealed RAF headquarters below street level, carved in the hard-packed earth forming the warehouse's foundation. It hadn't listed the location of the hidden door even though the Munich police had raised it on three separate occasions during the past ten years. Kurtzman's electronic eyes and ears had turned it up as a place Norbert Meineck had been known to frequent, even though he'd never been caught there.

The Executioner kept his weight evenly distributed as he circulated along the outer edges of the large floor. The hidden door was cut into the floor, a yard-by-yard-square section with cracks surrounding it that let the dust sift through. Once he'd located it, the area looked like an island in a dusty sea.

Kneeling beside the door, Bolan put down the MAC-10, then took a lock pick from the kit Kurtzman had provided. He slipped the curved end through the cracks and outlined the door, finding a trip wire of a concealed trap.

He kept the pressure against the trip as he raised the door. A pack of explosives was connected to the wire. Simple and deadly, but nothing once the mystery was gone.

Disarming the explosive, he eased himself down into the darkness, clinging to a wooden ladder hugging the dirt walls forming the narrow drop shaft. His shoulders brushed the walls of the tunnel, dislodging small puffs of dust. A raw, pungent odor of earth filled his lungs, constricting them for a moment.

He reached the end of the ladder, hanging suspended for a moment before easing himself down to arm's length. The ground met his feet. He swung the machine pistol forward, using his ears instead of his eyes to guide him.

A faint wisp of cigarette smoke wafted through the still air. An echo of displaced voices whispered across the thick silence surrounding him.

He moved forward, leaving the dead end of the tunnel behind him. The floor was surprisingly level, covered only by a small layer of loose soil. He released the holding strap over the Desert Eagle. Using it within the confines of the tunnel would be like unleashing raw thunder, but it carried an amount of psychological punch.

Bolan counted his steps automatically, keeping track of the direction of his mental map of the area. The tunnel lay in the direction of the river. Knowing that made the close walls somehow seem less oppressive.

He smelled the other man before he heard him. Old perspiration, deodorants and cologne clung to the man-scent that filled the tunnel. The Executioner flattened against the wall, dropping the MAC-10 on its sling at his side as his hand flashed for the Cold Steel Tanto combat knife sheathed in his boot.

Footsteps chuffed through the loose soil on the tunnel floor, punctuating the low rumble of voices coming toward him. As soon as the man brushed against Bolan, the Executioner took him. He snaked his free arm around the man's neck and drove the knife between the third and fourth ribs.

The guy convulsed, a scream dying even as he did, never getting past the arm that held him.

Bolan cleaned his knife on the man's shirt and went on. Even if these men weren't part of the group he was searching for, the only mercy in his heart consisted of quick death. The Red Army Faction had been responsible for the deaths of hundreds of people. Women and children were a favorite target because those deaths garnered public attention, spread their message to the world more quickly. The Executioner had received the same message the beginning of his lonely war from dozens of different sources. His response had never wavered, nor was it slow in coming.

A wooden door lay around the next turn, framed by a rectangle of weak yellow light. The voices sounded clearer now, speaking German.

Winding the sling of the machine pistol loosely around his wrist, the Executioner slid forward silently. He kicked out, striking the door two-thirds of the way up. Wood splintered, and the door fell forward. Bolan followed it in.

The three men gathered around a small table dived for weapons.

Subsonic rounds from the MAC-10 cut down the first man as he pulled an H&K 9 mm free of his belt. His body spilled backward, crushing a flimsy chair beneath him.

Bolan moved inside the room, triggering two more 3-round .45-caliber bursts. Both bursts took the second man full in the chest as his finger curled around the trigger of a mini-Uzi. Nine-millimeter bullets dug pockmarks from the earthen walls, clods dropping to the hard-packed floor. One of the rounds clipped the naked bulb and extinguished it.

Moving by memory and touch, Bolan pursued the third man, knowing his quarry had made it through the bolt-hole to the escape tunnel behind the wall of shelves. He tripped over the fallen boxes of rations and supplies. His shoulder slammed into the corner of the tunnel. Then he was through, operating on instinct and touch as he raced after the man.

A muzzle-flash winked to life ahead of him. The flash spread over the shooter's face, turning it almost vampire white. The earsplitting crash of thunder robbed the darkness of sound.

The bullet scored dirt from a tunnel wall and spilled it over Bolan's cheek. He wiped sand from his eye and rebounded suddenly as the tunnel jogged to the left. Charting his movements underground against his mental map, he figured the river was less than thirty feet away. Splashing noises sounded ahead of him, then the tunnel dropped away as his boots squelched through mud.

Off balance in the darkness, the Executioner went down, skidding through mud and spearing into the waiting water. Cold water covered his head as he tried to find solid footing. He came up gasping from the chill, his free hand scraping the ceiling of the tunnel only inches from the water's surface.

Pausing to listen, he heard nothing but the gentle slap of water against the earthen walls. Realizing the escape route was underwater and the man had already fled through it, he took a deep breath and went under. Precious seconds passed as he searched for the exit. Finding it, he returned for another breath, then dived deep with the MAC-10 slung around his neck.

His fingers bit into the mud as he pulled himself through the tunnel. Cold strings twisted across his hands and face. Touch told him they were roots from plants and trees. Something darted against his chest and was gone, letting him know he wasn't the only live thing in the tunnel. He trailed a hand overhead to mark his passage. The contact dropped away at the same time the slow river current pulled at him.

Ignoring the burning sensation in his lungs, he kicked free of the tunnel and angled for the surface.

His hearing returned as soon as he broke free of the water. The harsh barking of an automatic pistol greeted him. The bullets chewed through the water only a few feet away and started closing.

A brief impression from his peripheral vision let him know the RAF gunner had made shore. He let the water take him under rather than using the machine pistol to put the guy down. A quick five-count later, he resurfaced and swam for shore, twenty yards from where he'd been.

The shooter had invested the time in running, doubling back to the warehouse area.

Bolan knew he had precious little time to catch the man. If the shots hadn't called attention to the area, the man undoubtedly had a vehicle in the vicinity. The warrior came slogging out on the muddy bank and threw himself uphill, using his hands to aid him. He pushed himself, driving his feet hard against the ground.

When the RAF gunner turned and leveled his pistol, the Executioner flipped into a shoulder roll and pulled the MAC-10 into play as he came to his knees.

Bolan squeezed off a single round, aiming for the man's shoulder. The gunner came off his feet as the slug slammed into him. The Executioner was up at once, closing in as the man rolled over painfully and made frantic grabs for his lost weapon. Bolan kicked it away, meeting the guy's scared stare with the big muzzle of the MAC-10. "We're going to talk," he said in English.

"What do you want?" the man asked in broken English.

"Norbert Meineck."

"I do not know him."

Bolan knelt and swiftly frisked the man, keeping the MAC-10 out of reach. "Then I'm wasting my time." He raised the machine pistol meaningfully.

The man held up his hands. "Wait."

Bolan gave him a graveyard smile. "This heartbeat's all yours, guy, but you're going to have to earn the next one."

"I know him."

"Tell me where I can find him."

"He was not down there."

"I know that."

The man clasped a hand to his bleeding shoulder. "I do not know where he is."

"Then tell me where to find him."

Pain stained the man's features. "I do not know. Please do not kill me."

"Tell me about the hit on the safehouse in East Berlin a couple nights ago."

"I do not know anything."

"The Red Army Faction's getting the credit for it."

"It was not us. Meineck was in on it."

"That I already know." Bolan lifted the machine pistol, centering it between the man's eyes. "You're wasting my time."

The man blinked rapidly. "Meineck's part of a splinter group. They call themselves the Reunification Party Torch. He came by yesterday, trying to recruit some of our members."

"He didn't leave a name or a number where he could be reached?"

"No. He dropped out of sight about a month ago, along with some other people. We knew they had joined another group, but we did not know who. Then."

Bolan waited, knowing silence was his strongest threat.

"There was something else," the man said. Desperation gleamed in his eyes. "I know where Meineck and his group are going to be tonight."

Bolan ignored him. "Where are Meineck and his people getting the information on the agents they've killed?"

"I do not know. Meineck mentioned they had a source, but I got the impression he did not know, either."

The Executioner figured the man was telling the truth. Even if Norbert Meineck wasn't close to the actual top of the splinter group, he was at least close enough to recruit people. "What about the attack on the Karlsruhe banquet last night?"

"I do not know anything about it. I had heard the Russians were behind it."

"Where can I find Meineck?"

"A trade." The RAF man glanced at the barrel of the machine pistol. "A trade. My life for the information."

"I already have your life."

"I'd never tell you where Meineck is."

"You could be lying."

"No more than you."

"If you are," Bolan said in a wintery voice, "I'll make finding you a special project of mine."

"And if you are lying to me?"

Bolan gave him a thin grin. "You never know till you spin the wheel."

The man swallowed hard, closing his eyes as his Adam's apple bobbed up and down. "He bragged to me yesterday. Told me the next man they were going to execute was Viktor Ascherfeld."

"Who's he?"

"Ascherfeld is an ex-East German official, part of the deposed Communist regime. He lives in East Berlin. While he was in office, Ascherfeld bilked the East German government of millions of dollars."

"But Ascherfeld's not a member of a foreign espionage group."

"No."

"So their targets aren't always foreign agents?"

"I don't know. Meineck said they were going to make an example of him."

Bolan turned it over in his mind, trying to make sense of it. The Reunification Party Torch, if that's what it was really called, had access to sensitive information, weapons, money and people who could ease their rapid deployment in either Germany. Someone was networking their movements, planning their strikes, following a game plan that had to have been established months ago, but he didn't have a clue as to who was doing it or why it was being done. And the clock was running.

He pushed himself to his feet, pausing long enough to seize the man's weapon from the ground and hurl it into the river. He left the man alive because he'd given his word, and turned his steps toward the car that had come with Kurtzman's care package. The instincts of a trained hunter followed along in his mind, but this time he didn't know what to expect when he'd tracked the prey back to its lair.

"YOU'RE EARLIER than I'd expected," Kurtzman said.

"Got a break the first time out," Bolan said as he leaned into the phone booth.

"It happens."

"All too rarely."

Oktoberfest revelers paraded gaily through the streets, singing in off-key voices.

"What have you got?" Kurtzman asked.

"A splinter group of the RAF. They call themselves the Reunification Party Torch. I was told
they're the death squad hunting foreign agents."

"Meineck's tied in with them?"

"Yeah."

"I don't have anything on the RPT," the Bear replied. "Not even a rumor."

"The terrorist activity over here is pretty closed-
mouthed." Bolan tore a lid from a foam cup of coffee and took a sip. It warmed him despite the wet
blacksuit and the wind. "That's partly what keeps it
effective and partly what keeps it weakened."

"A show of strength only draws the competition."

"I know. See what you can find on Viktor Ascherfeld."

"Spelling?"

"Any way you want to."

"You're all heart, guy. You know how it is with
computers. They're the smartest things in the world—
as long as you hit them with the right question. And
spelling counts."

"Just be glad neatness doesn't."

Kurtzman growled good-naturedly. "I resent that
remark."

Bolan finished the coffee, glancing at the bronze
skin of the Mercedes the Stony Man computer expert
had provided. Thoughts of Firenze Falkenhayn
crowded into his mind until he banished them.

"Ah, Ascherfeld, Viktor. East German. Part of the
Communist regime that fell along with the Wall."

"That's the guy."

"Herr Ascherfeld's been a bad boy, Striker. He's lucky he's still got a whole skin." Kurtzman's fingers kept tapping.

"The RPT is supposed to change that tonight."

"What do you need from me?"

"An address where I can find him." Bolan reached inside his pocket for his war book. Kurtzman gave him an East Berlin address, and he checked it out against the maps in his map case, marking the way mentally without indicating it on the paper.

"I can go you one better than a home address, Striker. Apparently the Russians have been keeping tabs on their boy. I accessed a couple of field reports that got red-flagged during my search. From what I see here, Ascherfeld and his wife have reservations for nine o'clock tonight at Restaurant Moskau."

Bolan checked his watch. "I'm moving on it now. Let's hope they're fashionably late. How soon can I get some air transport?"

"When you get to the airport," Kurtzman said, "it'll be waiting on you. Under the Belasko name." The computer expert chuckled. "The way I got it figured, Striker, between the McKay cover, the Belasko cover, the name you originally entered West Berlin under and the two aliases I have set up for you for emergency extraction, you're five people visiting the country now."

"Yeah, well, let's hope the five of me are going to be enough."

FELIX SCHARNHORST SAT at the bar in Restaurant Moskau waiting for his latest target. He drank dark, sweet coffee that steamed when he breathed on it.

Norbert Meineck crossed the room and sat beside him. The bartender came over, and Meineck ordered a beer, looking at Scharnhorst self-consciously.

Scharnhorst blew on his coffee again, drawing in the steaming vapor, then taking a quick sip. He didn't care what the man drank. In the end Meineck and all the other RAF members he'd solicited to the cause would be nothing more than cannon fodder. Personally he felt that was more than they deserved.

"Where is he?" Meineck asked in a low voice. His eyes darted around the room.

"He will be here. Either quit staring around the room or go back to the car."

Meineck returned his attention to his beer. "Of course. You are right."

Scharnhorst listened to the thrumming that resonated within him, tightening it and playing it the way he'd seen master violinists do in concerts.

"A bomb would have been better," Meineck said. "There would have been no chance of anyone getting caught."

"If everyone does as they are supposed to," Scharnhorst replied, "no one will be caught."

"The other men, the spies, we killed them without risk to ourselves," Meineck protested.

"Tell that to Elias and the men who fell under the CIA agent's bullets two nights ago."

"That was different. There was no choice in how we took those men. With Ascherfeld, we could strike at his home. A bomb. I'm very good with those."

"No." Scharnhorst's tone was unrelenting. He tried to keep his dislike for the other man out of it. "It will be done this way, and a message will be left for all men like him. They are done with robbing and raping our country. There's a new future coming for us, and no one will stand in its way."

A beep sounded in Scharnhorst's ear. He checked his watch. It was 9:37.

"Ascherfeld?" Meineck whispered.

"Yes. Take your place."

Meineck emptied his beer stein and left the bar.

Scharnhorst went on sipping his coffee, watching the main entrance in the mirror against the wall in front of him. The bar area was small, with tiny square tables covered with brown linens packed close together. Candlelight fluttered from the tables across the floor. Oil lamps hung from the walls. Russian dialects were almost as prevalent as East German ones.

Viktor Ascherfeld came through the door accompanied by three bodyguards and his wife. The man was obese. Even the cut of his expensive suit couldn't hide his enormous girth. Beside him, his wife looked elfin small, dressed in white with a white fur draping her shoulders. Like her husband's, her hair was pale blond, but where Ascherfeld's was clipped short and neat, hers was filled with curling body that caught the candlelight.

The guards were dressed in cheap suits and looked as if they'd come off a factory line specializing in firm chin lines and broad shoulders. Scharnhorst's practiced eye didn't miss the weapons leathered under their arms.

A small, dapper host in black greeted them. An exchange of conversation, in Russian, followed, then Ascherfeld and his party were led across the floor to the restaurant section.

Five more electronic beeps sounded in Scharnhorst's ear, letting him know at least five more men
waited outside. Scharnhorst finished his coffee and
drifted in Ascherfeld's wake like a shark trailing a
chum boat. Eight men, and possibly more, all to cover
Ascherfeld's night out. Meineck hadn't seen the truth
that taking the man was easier once he was out of his
fortress. And the plan Scharnhorst followed demanded that the kill be sure and clean.

He kept to the shadows lining the walls of the restaurant area as he'd been trained, taking a seat by
himself to the rear. He blew out the candle on his table and waited as Ascherfeld and his entourage took
their places. The guards weren't allowed to eat with
their boss. That was the second mistake the man had
made. The first had been in deciding to come out of
his hiding place at all.

Reaching under his jacket, Scharnhorst tapped on
the signaling device at his belt. An inquiry, beeped at
a higher frequency than the other men, sounded in his
ear. It was answered quickly as the previous five beeps
repeated themselves.

A waitress came by and addressed him in Russian.

Scharnhorst replied in German, ordering a Kiever
cutlet and coffee. She thanked him in German, flashed
a brief smile and went on her way. He continued
watching Ascherfeld, marking time until his men positioned themselves outside. Twenty minutes would be
cutting it close with the kind of men he'd been able to
enlist. But there were some, not like Meineck, who
were professionals and worked for the money involved and not a misguided patriotic fervor. Still, they
needed the RAF people for cover.

A rapid tattoo of electronic beeps rattled into his ear, signaling a warning. The waitress brought his coffee. He used her presence to mask his inspection of the main entranceway.

The man who followed the host was the CIA agent who'd escaped the attack on the safehouse. Scharnhorst smiled to himself as the intensity of the thrumming inside him increased. Then he saw the waitress smile as she mistakenly thought the expression was directed at her. She reached into her apron and brought out a lighter. He caught her hands as she tried to light the extinguished candle.

"No," he said quietly, "please. The smoke bothers my eyes."

"As you will," she replied, then drifted away.

Scharnhorst looked back for the CIA agent. The man had disappeared somewhere in the darkness of the restaurant. He cursed inwardly. The agent couldn't know about him without tripping the sensitive lines they'd covered him with. For the man to be there tonight meant he'd penetrated the mission in some other way. Scharnhorst had no doubt that Meineck's people were the root of his present problem. He closed his hand around the mini-Uzi hanging under his arm. His watch's second hand started its sweep on the last minute.

8

"May I take your coat?" the young waitress asked as she led the Executioner into the dining area.

"No, thank you," Bolan replied as he finished unzipping the brown bomber jacket. The interior of Restaurant Moskau was dimly lighted, relying almost totally on candles at the individual tables. He recognized Viktor Ascherfeld and his wife from the photos Kurtzman faxed to the waiting plane that dropped him into Berlin.

"Do you have a preference, sir?"

"Along the wall, thanks. I'll be dining alone."

"Of course."

Ascherfeld and his group sat near the curtained stage area. The ex-German official dined with his wife and was presently engaged in animated conversation with her. His three bodyguards sat together at a table separating him from the rest of the diners.

Bolan kept his jacket on as he sat. The Desert Eagle felt solid and dependable under his left arm. His combat senses were already tingling.

"Would you like something to drink?" the waitress asked as she left a menu with him.

"Lager."

She nodded and moved away.

Besides the bodyguards, the warrior also tagged a two-man Russian team who were keeping Ascherfeld under surveillance. They sat farther back to the left of the stage area at an unlighted table. Bolan recognized the older man as Yegor Paputin, a senior field agent who'd been in the briefing files provided by Brognola.

According to the big Fed's files, Paputin was one of the cooler heads operating in the Berlin sector. The West German government evidently thought so, as well. They'd used Paputin a number of times to work out internal strife between the Germanys. The agent was in his sixties, bald and slightly overweight, gunmetal gray eyes almost hidden under shaggy silver eyebrows. His partner was younger, with an ineffectual look about him.

Wondering if the Russian agents were operating off of similar Intel or if their interest in Ascherfeld was strictly routine, Bolan scanned through the rest of the crowd. Norbert Meineck wasn't visible. Only a few of the restaurant's patrons weren't suspect. With the destruction of the wall, Restaurant Moskau had become a place for clandestine deals revolving around the black market that bootlegged goods into Eastern Europe.

The curtains over the postage-stamp-size stage parted, drawing back to the sides to drop a rectangle of light over the front tables. Viktor Ascherfeld was front and center. The fat man turned in his chair, smiling as the band behind the curtains came to life with a blast of brass and a rattle of drums and cymbals.

The woman singer advanced on the microphone only to be brushed out of the way by a masked gunman carrying an H&K MP-5. The submachine gun extinguished the music and ensuing screams as it chattered to life.

The steady stream of 9 mm rounds chewed across Ascherfeld's table, knocking the man and his wife to the ground. Their white clothes became ragged twists of scarlet as broken dishes and glasses showered over the surrounding tables.

Even as the first gunner's magazine ran dry, a second attacker fell in at his side. Screams punctuated the roar of the submachine gun as the rounds pursued the dodging bodyguards struggling to bring their weapons into play.

Bolan's .44 cleared leather as he rolled into the aisle. His initial round caught the second gunner in the shoulder, spinning the man and directing the MP-5's line of fire in a blistering arc across the ceiling. Chunks of acoustic tile and fluorescent light tube fragments showered to the floor.

The Executioner's second shot put the man down permanently with a bullet through the heart. Then the warrior was up and scuffling through the human tide driven by sudden fear that tried to sweep him back toward the entrance doors. He reached for the man closest to him, grabbed the guy's collar and yanked. The man stumbled to one side, allowing Bolan the distance he needed to break through the line.

The first assassin lowered his recharged weapon as Bolan settled the big Desert Eagle in a two-fisted Weaver's grip. He was aware of more submachine guns joining the first two, completing the chaos inside the restaurant and driving the Russian agents under cover. Bullets struck miniature flares as they glanced off of metal equipment and silverware scattered across the tables.

A line of 9 mm rounds slashed through the air at the warrior's side as he reached target acquisition. He squeezed the .44's trigger, and the hollowpoint bullet struck the RPT gunner just above the bridge of his nose. The impact blew the assassin back, driving the corpse into a tangled heap with the drums.

Going to ground, Bolan took up a position behind an overturned table. He felt the vibration of bullets striking the underside of the table against his back. None of them made it through.

Another blaze of autofire ripped holes in the far wall near the entrance, closing in on the group of people trying to squeeze through the doors all at once.

Estimating the gunner's probable position, Bolan rolled onto his knees as he lifted the Desert Eagle. He spotted two men. One, dressed as the others had been, was working the H&K subgun. The man at his side tracked a handgun onto the Executioner's position.

Bolan had a brief impression of the gunner's large size, the black duster that swirled around him and the muzzle-flash of the man's weapon even as his finger tightened on the .44 Magnum's trigger.

The warrior pulled two shots in rapid fire, not bothering with actual sighting, relying on his honed instincts. Both rounds struck the man just below the throat, where undercover bulletproof armor wasn't available.

Then Bolan felt a red-hot stinger stab into his neck. Unable to maintain his balance he went down, blood sliding down his back and shoulder.

His arm numb from the impact, he transferred the .44 between his knees, then reached inside his jacket for a smoke grenade. Police sirens wailed. He knew it wouldn't be long before the Vopos arrived.

He pulled the pin and flipped the grenade toward the front of the restaurant. It landed short of the stage, well out of reach of the RPT members. He gripped the butt of his weapon as the hollow pop of the grenade sounded.

A cloud of inky darkness spread across the front of the stage, made even blacker by the spotlights.

Forcing himself to his feet, Bolan hunkered down as he crossed the room to Ascherfeld's table. A thick German voice ordered the gunmen from the room. The Executioner had no trouble recognizing the orders, nor the crisp military way they were delivered. His shoulder hurt like hell as he made his fingers respond, placing them against Ascherfeld's jugular, then that of his wife. Both were dead.

Building the restaurant mentally from his brief recon before entering the battle zone, he guessed at the RPT's most obvious escape route. Pain racked his neck and arm as he stepped onto the stage into the thickest part of the billowing smoke cloud.

Bolan shoved the dead gunner out of the way and stepped through the wreckage of the drum set. An authoritative voice rang out behind him, ordering him to stop.

The warrior stepped through the ripped folds of the curtains across the back of the stage, then pulled them behind him as he broke into a trot. He gritted his teeth against the fire blazing in his shoulder.

The narrow walkway behind the stage led into the kitchen area. Gleaming pots, pans and utensils hung on the stark white walls. Most of the smoke bomb's discharge had been kept from the kitchen by the curtains. Three white-clothed kitchen workers lay on the red-tiled floor with their hands over their heads. A fourth lay in the open space leading to the back door, in the spread-eagle position only death produced. Three bullet holes climbed his spine, powder burns testifying to how close his killer had been.

Bolan leaped over the body, pausing only momentarily at the side of the open door as he raised the Desert Eagle. He whirled, tracking the big .44 out before him as cold wind sliced into his face. Police commands in German echoed behind him, punctuated by the sound of running feet. He swept the automatic from side to side, finding no snipers waiting.

Snugging his hand into his jacket pocket, he took some of the pressure off his injured arm as he gave pursuit.

The alley was narrow, ringing with the sound of thudding boots, harsh voices filled with urgency and car engines firing up.

The warrior forced greater effort from his body, lifting his legs high and driving them down as he approached the sudden corner of the alley. He slammed his back against the wall as he brought up the .44. When he spun around the corner, all he saw were the brief flickers of brake lights as the escape vehicles powered away. A heartbeat later only gray wisps of exhaust remained.

"THEY GOT ASCHERFELD," Bolan said without preamble. He used a public phone only a few blocks from the airport where the small plane waited to ferry him back to Munich.

"Anything I can do from this end?" Kurtzman asked.

"Stay with the Ascherfeld investigation. The East German police are already at the scene. They might turn up something. The RPT left a few bodies of their own tonight. I want to know who they are."

"Any idea what I'm looking for?"

Bolan sighed. The shoulder still throbbed. Frustration chafed at him. The numbers on the operation were gearing up, signaling the nearness to an end he didn't even have in his sights yet. He wasn't sure how much time remained before the hit team closed up shop and walked away winners.

"The Ascherfeld hit doesn't scan, Aaron. Taking the supposed nature of the Reunification Party Torch into consideration, I can buy the strikes against foreign agents."

"But Ascherfeld doesn't fit."

"No."

"Still doesn't narrow the field for me. I can spend hours poking through background histories and cop reports and still not have a damn thing you can use when the dust clears."

"Let me see if I can narrow it for you," Bolan said. "The only reasons whoever's behind the RPT would hit Ascherfeld, would fall within two categories. Either to shut Ascherfeld up because he knew too much, or to create a set of circumstances that would be beneficial to the guy calling the shots. Ascherfeld didn't act like a man with any new worries, so I'm ruling the first scenario out. If it scans later, we can investigate."

"So what would prove beneficial to the RPT?"

Bolan answered without hesitation. "The money."

"Right," Kurtzman said with sudden enthusiasm. Keyboard clacking sounded over the phone.

Adjusting the receiver under his chin, Bolan added another compress to his neck injury. The bleeding had almost stopped. From the quick glance he'd been able to give it, the wound didn't appear to be more than superficial. The numbness had already passed.

"Once things start getting boiled down to the cash involved, generally you can get a handle on things quicker. How much money was Ascherfeld sitting on?"

"Millions, Striker. Ascherfeld had a long time to operate."

"What about locating it?"

"I've already got a line on some of his investments. The new East German government has prowled around with his records for months now, but they didn't turn up anything substantial. Nothing Ascherfeld didn't feel comfortable with giving them. However, what I turned up on my own is something else again. As much as Barb and I have to do in the way of exchanging political secrets behind closed doors for favors we need, this was something I was saving for a rainy day."

Barbara Price was mission controller for Stony Man Farm.

"Can you track the money?"

"Given sufficient lead time and the fact that they don't notice I'm sniffing around, sure."

"Stay with it. Keep me informed on what the Vopos turn up at the scene, but I'm betting it'll be nothing. The important thing will be finding out who wanted the money. Once we have the 'who,' the 'why' should follow in short order. Then, maybe everything else will drop into view and we can see what we need to do to set things right." He broke the connection.

"MR. MCKAY."

Bolan looked at Rachelle Moreau in the darkness. She sat alone at an outside table on the elegant Karlsruhe lawn. Her cheeks were reddened from the brisk wind, and her blond hair had a blown look about it that contained more sex appeal than tangles. She sat wrapped in a long coat, her legs drawn up inside it.

"Waiting on someone?" he asked as he stopped before her. "Should I continue to call you Rachelle, or would Firenze be more appropriate?"

She looked up at him coolly. "In front of the others I'd appreciate it if we continued with the deception." She gave him a meaningful stare. "It would save a lot of questions neither one of us wants to answer."

"Maybe I'm ready to take that chance. Karlsruhe might be more enthusiastic about harboring someone with CIA connections than someone who's a French spy."

She shook her head and brushed her hair from her face. The moonlight was kind to her subdued beauty, and Bolan couldn't help noticing the effect. "If you were ready for a confrontation like that, you wouldn't be here. Either Herr Karlsruhe would be tipped off about me quietly and I would be taken away, or one of your CIA associates would arrange an 'accident' to happen to me."

"It could still happen."

"I'll take that chance." Falkenhayn uncurled her feet and stood. "You forget I've seen you in action. Subtlety might be known to you, but you prefer a course that's straight and true. An economy of movement that's more suited to the professional soldier than to someone in the espionage field." She raised an eyebrow. "I'll remain in place until you're more sure of me. Or until I decide to vanish on my own."

"You're very sure of yourself."

"Aren't you?"

Bolan smiled but didn't reply. The woman's aggressive behavior irritated him, but he couldn't help respecting her for it. The business she was in stayed nasty. There were no good sides to it. The honesty with which she faced it must have made for many sleepless nights.

"You're bleeding," she said. "We'd better get inside before someone notices."

Glancing down at his palm, Bolan saw the thin line of blood trickling between his fingers onto the green grass. There hadn't been any time to properly care for the wound during the short flight into Munich. A change of dressing had been the most he could manage.

He wiped his hand on the tissue she provided, kept it balled inside his fist and followed her inside the house.

The staff security people had already been briefed about him, and the warrior recognized a few familiar faces among them. Evidently the new status granted by Karlsruhe had filtered quickly through the ranks. There were polite inquiries about his needs and nothing more.

Falkenhayn touched his shoulder as he keyed the lock of his door. "Leave it open," she said. "I'll get some things from my room and I'll be right back."

Bolan nodded and passed through. He undressed in the bathroom, left the door open and started a shower. Only the shirt he'd been wearing had soaked up blood. The traces on his jacket's liner were small pools and would escape all but direct examination.

The wound at the side of his neck held the dulled throbbing of beestings. A brief glance in the fogged mirror above the sink showed him it needed medical attention if it was going to heal properly. There would be no time tonight, but perhaps something could be arranged through Brognola tomorrow.

He closed his eyes and shampooed his hair one-handed, finishing up with a needle-jet spray of cold water that raised goose bumps all over his flesh. He kept the wound away from the brunt of it as blood and soapsuds sluiced down the drain.

Falkenhayn handed him a towel as he got out.

The French agent had shed the coat, revealing the lime-colored blouse and short white skirt she had on underneath. The smell of her perfume and her natural feminine charms tugged at Bolan's senses.

"You need stitches," she said, glancing at his neck with a critical eye. "At least three, maybe four. Otherwise you'll never get it to close properly." She held up a small black pouch. "If you'll allow me, I can take care of it. I've had some experience with injuries."

Wrapping the towel around his waist, the warrior sat on the edge of the tub. It was a matter of trust, and it was a matter of life and death when everything was cut to the chase. He felt her intentions were honest and he'd learned to follow his instincts.

"Surgical thread," Falkenhayn said as she produced a spool. "It's white so it doesn't attract attention. Like this, it looks like something every woman would carry to replace a button in case of a sartorial emergency. The other tubes I have here are all mislabeled as cosmetics, but they contain medicine." She smiled. "However, I don't have anything resembling local anesthetic."

"It's okay," Bolan replied.

She nodded briefly. "I can see you've had experience with this sort of quick-fix repair work. I was worried about my own skill at needlepoint until I saw some of the handiwork you've already had."

"Some of it wasn't done under optimum conditions."

"I noticed." She threaded her needle expertly, then retrieved a pair of small scissors from the pouch. Leaning forward, she joined the torn pieces of flesh together with her fingertips. "Ready?"

"Ready." Bolan took his mind away from the immediate pain, focusing on the nearness of the woman and cutting the agony off at the knees until it was only a frantic drumbeat in a dim recess of his senses. He kept his eyes open, watching the smooth contours of her face. The scent of her filled his lungs. The warmth of her soaked into his skin and melted away the chill of the shower.

"You're not regulation Agency material," Falkenhayn said as she worked to tie off the first stitch. "I don't know who you are yet, but that I do know. None of Scott's men would let me this close to them."

"Yeah, but I know this works two ways. This isn't strictly a Florence Nightingale act here. You're wondering where I've been and what I've been up to."

She smiled. "Touché, Mr. McKay. There was nothing in your pockets."

"No."

"You're a very careful man."

"You're working on evidence to the contrary."

"Wrong. This wound tells me you were involved in some kind of heavy engagement tonight, not a one-on-one affair. Somewhere. With my sources, I'll know where by morning."

"Maybe."

She shrugged as she finished the last stitch. "Maybe. And if I don't, perhaps I've aided a compatriot. See, that's the kind of game we're in here—you never know who your friends are until you find them there. But there are no assurances they will remain friendly. The next day those same acquaintances could be looking for you to drop your body in the nearest convenient hole and cover you over."

She applied thick gel from one of the tubes and smeared it over the wound, then added a white gauze bandage. "Personally I don't want to see the day come when I have to undo all the work I've just finished." She put all her supplies back in the pouch. "Just so you'll know, if it comes down to that—I will."

"I never had a doubt about it."

She quirked her lips in a tired smile, allowing the warrior a brief peek at the worn soul underneath the hard surface before she hid it away again. "I would give you the speech about how you're not supposed to get the wound wet over the next few days and how you shouldn't strain it, but it would be wasted breath. You've evidently heard it all before."

"Yeah. It's not always a pleasant world out there."

"Especially not when you're trying to survive around its harder edges." She turned to go, pausing at the door long enough to say "Good night, McKay."

Bolan took the .45 from the soap dish inside the shower stall and carried it into the bedroom. He dressed in a pair of gym shorts, then painfully pulled on a white T-shirt over his head to cover the bandage in case any of the house staff came in before he was up in the morning.

He switched off the bedside lamp and lay on his back, his injured arm placed loosely across his chest to alleviate any stress. He tucked the .45 under his pillow within easy reach. Relaxing his breathing, he willed sleep to come with the soldier's ability that would never leave him.

Firenze Falkenhayn was a cipher. The thought gnawed at the ragged edges of his conscious mind. The scent and feel of her wouldn't leave him. She could be a deadly foe, yet a compassionate woman, as well. It was that same duality of nature within the human animal that had allowed the jungles of Vietnam to give birth to the Executioner and Sergeant Mercy. They were the same man, too.

And the warrior was willing to give the lady that. Being trained as a predator didn't always burn away the compassion.

Still, with what he'd learned tonight—that the RPT wasn't just an organization working against political control through foreign agents and might possibly have mercenary interests, as well—Falkenhayn became a primary suspect in the scheme of things.

Already confirmed were her ties to the French counterterrorist group and a supposed sellout to the CIA. There was no way of knowing where her ultimate loyalty lay. But the warrior had a feeling wherever it was, it was there for keeps.

Just as his was. He couldn't help but hope their paths would run parallel without crossing. Killing her wasn't something he'd look forward to. But if push came to shove, he wouldn't hesitate, either. He had a feeling the lady knew that, too.

"THAT OUR BOY?"

Falkenhayn blinked against the noonday sun's reflection in John Scott's mirrored sunglasses. The CIA section chief wore a woolen suit that protected him from the chill wind sweeping across the Theresienwiese and successfully covered the shoulder holster with the .41 Dan Wesson Magnum she knew from his file that he favored. He was fair headed, with sharp angular features that blended him in well with the crowd filling the Oktoberfest celebration.

"McKay?" she asked. She wore a blouse, American jeans and an artificial fur coat that dropped to midthigh. A scarf around her head and dark sunglasses kept most of the wind from her face.

"Belasko," Scott said. "That's the ID I turned up on him. He's some kind of hotshot within Intelligence circles. A real wild card. The guy's jacket reads like the Lone Ranger. He rides into town, takes down an operation and fades before the first round of kudos hits the wire."

"You don't know him?" she asked.

The Oktoberfest festival filled the temporary and permanent buildings in Ausstellungspark. Gaily colored Bavarian marching bands tuned up their instruments as they chatted with one another and readied themselves for the big parade that would start within moments. Pennants and flags whipped and cracked in the crisp breeze.

The large beer halls subsidized by the local breweries were capable of housing several thousand guests each. Many of the people strolling through the packed alleys and byways formed between the buildings and tents and wooden stands carried foaming mugs of whichever local brew they favored. The whole atmosphere was charged with a feeling of fast and furious good fun.

Motorized floats and horse-drawn floats were being lined up now, escorted by sharp-dressed members of the local police departments. News helicopters rattled through the blue skies, weaving dragonfly-shaped shadows across the crowds. The ninety-eight-foot bronze statue of Bavaria towered over all. Faces of excited visitors pressed against the small windows of the head.

"Not from Adam."

Besides the usual amount of revelry this year, Oktoberfest also played host to the committee of West and East German businessmen seeking to negotiate a financial merger for the two economies.

The surviving members of that group, Falkenhayn silently amended. Despite the tragic events of the previous twenty-four hours and the fact that today was Sunday, Karlesruhe had convinced the members to continue as planned as a show of strength against their unknown enenies.

"There," Falkenhayn said as she found Bolan. She felt a twinge of guilt for pointing him out but quickly put it away.

The big man stood along an outer fringe of the reporters clustered around the stage section Karlsruhe had reserved for their public address. A phalanx of international television cameras were arranged before the stage. Reporters conferred with their cameramen, oblivious to the partying going on around them.

Falkenhayn would have been with them if Scott hadn't set up this meeting. As it was, she risked her cover if somebody made her with the CIA man.

"Guy doesn't look like so much," the section chief said.

She didn't say anything. It was American bravado speaking, nothing more.

McKay wore a dark suit and black sunglasses that merged him with the businessmen and their bodyguards. At his side was an older, redheaded woman wielding a 35 mm camera with grim efficiency. Falkenhayn remembered the woman's name with difficulty. Peg Morelund was some kind of photojournalist working on spec for a national newsmagazine based in New York.

Horns blew as the parade floats shifted, getting ready for their cue. Horses stamped as streams of gray mist shot out their nostrils. Harness wear, instruments and transmission gears all clanked away as everyone idled in readiness.

"Can you get close to him?" Scott asked suddenly.

"How do you mean?"

"You know exactly what I mean, Orchid," he replied in a harsh voice, using her cover name.

"Yes."

Scott adjusted his tie, shifting the slim briefcase in his hand forward so it would be noticeable. "My superiors have got an uneasy feeling about a wild card like Belasko in the stew. Things seemed to have become increasingly complicated since his arrival."

"I agree." Falkenhayn couldn't help thinking that an increase in confusion during the progression of an especially knotty operation was sometimes like the darkness of night before the dawn.

"My superiors want him out of the way," Scott went on.

Falkenhayn looked at him only to be kept away from his thoughts by the mirrored lenses of his sunglasses.

"And they're prepared to pay handsomely for it. I've got twenty-five thousand dollars inside this case."

She didn't reply for a moment, weighing all the options. With so many alliances one undisclosed commitment could leave her in a precarious position with a number of people and agencies. "McKay is a dangerous man," she said. "I've seen him in action."

Scott showed her a mirthless smile. "You get another twenty-five thou once your target's confirmed down."

"Thirty-five."

Some of the smile left his face. He nudged the mirror sunglasses farther up his nose with a forefinger. "Okay, babe, but I want this guy put down soon, understand?"

"Yes."

Scott passed over the briefcase.

She curled her fingers around the handle, glad she wore gloves so she didn't have any real physical contact with the man.

The CIA section chief walked away without another word.

Falkenhayn felt the heaviness of the money inside the briefcase, mirroring the heaviness of the complexities facing her with her chosen and unchosen roles. A quick visual scan assured her no detonating devices were on the outside of the case.

The parade of floats began as she made her way back to her car to drop off the briefcase. Scott's behavior confused her. She could believe that someone in the Company believed McKay to be a threat as a loose cannon. And she could believe that an order could be handed down so quickly to have the man removed from the mission. American agencies didn't hesitate to cull from their own ranks. Too often they found double and triple agents within their membership.

The thought chased a cool thrill down her spine as she considered her own tenuous position.

The thing that bothered her was Scott's immediate agreement to the sum she'd mentioned. Either McKay really was considered as a big threat by someone, or the CIA intended to terminate their involvement with her once she'd succeeded. And her with it.

"MY GOD," Peg Morelund said with genuine feeling, "I've never seen anything like this. Have you?"

"Only once," Bolan replied.

The woman referred to the stream of floats navigating through the narrow street the Munich policemen had managed to carve from the surrounding crowd. The floats came in an endless variety. Some were in the shape of people, while others depicted forest scenes from fantasy or actual bits of history. Decked out in multicolored streamers and ribbons, covered with balloons of all sizes and crowded by people wearing costumes to match each individual float, they were the center of attention.

Bands and youth groups marched between the floats. The air crackled with the energetic music. Microphones swept singing voices over the crowds, where the words were picked up and added to as the listeners joined in.

"When?" Morelund asked.

Bolan looked at her.

"When did you see this before?" The woman worked her camera in a frenzy. The automatic winder seemed to be making constant noise as the film advanced.

"I was in the Army," Bolan replied. It was the truth, even for the McKay background. "I spent part of a tour in Germany."

"Must have been some time ago." Morelund looked up quickly from her camera. "No offense."

"None taken." Bolan shifted, keeping his attention on the gathered group of German businessmen applauding the parade of floats. It spoke volumes about the amount of charisma Jeorg Karlsruhe generated among the financial sectors that most of his invited guests had shown up for the meeting in spite of yesterday's events.

Bolan had the .45 holstered against his spine. His shoulder still felt stiff and creaky, but it wasn't as bad as it could have been. Falkenhayn's ministrations had helped. He searched for her through the crowd but couldn't find her. It wasn't surprising. In the open, near the center of the celebration, there were too many other things to keep watch over. And Falkenhayn had her own skills with fading into the background even as he did.

Returning his gaze to Karlsruhe, he watched the businessman converse with the other men around him. Karlsruhe's hands rested heavily on the silver-headed cane. Bodyguards fidgeted nervously, the pomp and clamor having evidently already shaken their confidence.

The warrior figured that was a good thing. It would serve to keep the men on their toes. No matter how much protection was put on a person, a determined assassin could still put a target down before being detected. Bolan knew the game from both sides of the gun.

A string of rifle shots popped through the festive noises, driving everyone into sudden action. Hoarse screams and shouts disrupted the singing. Musical instruments clattered to the ground as the musicians abandoned them.

"Sniper!" was a rallying yell that echoed in a half-dozen languages.

Bolan drew the Smith & Wesson as he grabbed for the back of Morelund's jacket and pulled her to the ground.

"Up there!" the photojournalist screamed. She pointed toward a tent less than two hundred yards away.

Knowing he could never make the distance through the confusion of the crowd, Bolan wheeled and hustled back toward the group surrounding Karlsruhe's position. One of the security guards backed him off with a gun. "What happened?" the warrior asked.

"Herr Karlsruhe was shot," the guard said, continuing to back the Executioner away. The rest of the security team formed a flying wedge around the man and started for the armored limousine parked behind the stage area.

"How is he?"

"He will be fine. We are very fortunate. Herr Karlsruhe wore his bulletproof vest. Now, please stay back, Herr McKay. We must get him out of here."

Bolan nodded and cleared off. There was nothing he could do that Karlsruhe's people couldn't take care of. He glanced back at the tent. Already squads of Munich policemen were surrounding the area. The way they set up a quick blitz in all four directions told him the assassin had already dropped into hiding.

He looked for Falkenhayn, saw her standing to the left almost twenty yards away. Her face seemed hard and serious around the dark lenses of her sunglasses.

She turned away and melted into the throng of people surrounding her.

"Hey, Mike."

Bolan helped Peg Morelund to her feet. The woman beamed happily. She held up her camera in triumph.

"Think you know enough German to help me find some darkroom equipment?"

9

"I *did* get the bastard's picture."

Bolan peered over Morelund's shoulder as she held the print under the developing solution with a pair of plastic tongs. The picture started out as a series of whites, grays and blacks, and deepened in texture and intensity as color was added.

They stood huddled in the large bathroom of a rented hotel suite in downtown Munich. Pans of chemical solutions covered the available table space. Thumbtacks secured two separate lengths of twine that crisscrossed the room. Plastic clothes pins held 8 × 10 prints in haphazard fashion. A collection of postage-stamp-size negatives were taped to the mirror in long strips.

"Here it is," the photojournalist said, pulling the print from the solution with the tongs.

Bolan leaned forward, unable to see anything more than the stark black-and-white effect of the color picture with the red light filling the room.

The photo showed the top of the tent the sniper had used as a shooting platform. A puff of gray smoke was frozen just above the shooter's head. The man was too small and too far away to be identified.

"Can you blow it up?"

"Sure." Morelund bent to the task, moving back to the negatives and the developing pans.

Bolan rolled his head from side to side to loosen the muscles, taking care with the left side. It was almost three hours after the sniping incident, approaching two o'clock in the afternoon. It had taken almost an hour to get free of the Oktoberfest traffic, and assorted law-enforcement agencies, and find a hotel room. Brognola had aided with the darkroom equipment.

"Remember our agreement," Morelund said. "I get first dibs on moving the photos and the story."

"It's all yours," Bolan replied. "I'm just interested in the guy behind the gun."

"Somehow I'm beginning to think your *real* story would be as good as what we're looking at here."

"Maybe. But that's one you won't get."

She grinned at him, looking twenty years younger while flushed with excitement. "I love a challenge almost as much as I love a mystery, McKay, so don't tempt an old lady too much."

He returned the smile. There was something about watching over her shoulder as she worked that slowed down the pace of the mission for him and gave him a brief sense of ease. Things were still hanging fire, true, but carrying the ball was in her hands for the moment. Until she came up with something solid or came up empty, he was sidelined for the moment. Police officials in the area made things too hot for outside interference.

He freshened their coffee, then picked up the phone when it rang. "Yeah."

"Me," Brognola said. "Anything?"

"Something. We're still working it."

"The sniper?"

"On film, but it needs to be enlarged before we can try to make a positive ID."

"From what I've been able to pick up, your lady's the only one who photographed the sniper. You'll let me know as soon as you have anything?"

"Sure." Bolan switched gears, knowing something was disturbing the big Fed. "How's Karlsruhe?"

"Bruised. Pissed. He's almost ready to declare war on the Russians."

"Why?"

"The gun they found was a Russian sniper make. Direct from Spetsnaz weapons lockers."

"Do the German governments know that?"

"Not yet. But it's only a matter of time."

"The hitter left the weapon behind?"

"Wiped clean of prints. Like a pointing finger."

"And their in-town players?"

"Staying as clear of the area as they can." Brognola cleared his throat. "The Man wants to set up a meet between you and the local Russian team. Since they're going to have to run a low profile, he thought it might be a good idea to take a peek at what they've got in their portfolio."

"At whatever they're willing to share."

"There's that." Brognola hesitated. "They've come across with one interesting tidbit, though, Striker. They fingered the Falkenhayn woman as an East German mole in French employ."

"And she's supposed to be doubling as a CIA informant."

"Yeah. Getting nasty, isn't it?"

"It already has been."

"So the Russians might be our next big line for a counteroffensive against whoever's pulling the strings on this little frame job. The problem is they're only available for a one-time last-ditch effort before the German governments ask them to go home."

"And the CIA's effectively sidelined as long as we leave the lady in play."

"Yeah. Getting down to the bone, leaving the pickings down to slim and none. I can get some directions through channels I have open to me. Maybe get Scott and his boys to scoop Falkenhayn up and sit on her."

"If you do that, there's no telling what chain of events you're liable to kick into motion."

"I know. I just wanted you to know you weren't trapped by the present scenario."

"I've got some latitude. Let me play out the string I've got before we cash it in."

"It's your call, guy. You've got the field."

Morelund turned around suddenly, holding up a dripping print. "I've got it."

Bolan told Brognola to hold on as he bent forward to survey the woman's results. The image had been blown up four or five times and was centered almost on the sniper. Even with the face partially blocked by the scope, Bolan recognized the man at once as being the leader of the RPT team that had tagged Ascherfeld. He clapped Morelund on the shoulder in silent congratulations. "Can you print me a half-dozen copies of that?"

"Yes."

"And crop everything out but the face?"

"Consider it done."

Bolan stepped back and raised the receiver up again. "We've got a face."

"Great. I'll get Aaron working on it as soon as you can make a drop."

"The guy in the photo is the same one who fronted the hit on the target in East Berlin last night."

"The guy gets around."

"True, but I have to wonder how the RPT's interest in killing foreign agents in the Germanys ties in with the hit on a known ex-East German official and planned assassinations of businessmen supposed to be working for economic reunification."

"We might have to wait to see how everything stacks up after the final washout."

"Yeah. I'll drop these pictures as soon as I can. Set up the meet with the other team for sometime early this evening. We're approaching meltdown on this soon, and I want a handle on it before then." Bolan caught Morelund's eye. "One other thing."

"What?"

"I've got a lady here who's going to need phone and fax lines to New York within the next hour. I told her we could fix her up through diplomatic channels."

"Done. Stay frosty, big guy." Brognola broke the connection.

"You're pretty good at double-talk," Morelund said over her shoulder.

"Comes with the territory."

"And you're not about to let me know what territory that is."

"No. You've already got one scoop today. A lot of reporters will be as envious as hell by morning."

"It'll probably only last until tomorrow afternoon's headlines."

Bolan sipped his coffee in silence as he watched the woman put the first of the copies into the finishing vat. He stared into the sniper's face, willing himself to know the man the next time their paths crossed. There would be no putting the man down without violence. The assassin had the look of a man who enjoyed his job.

Abruptly the image changed in his mind, transposing Firenze Falkenhayn's face over the sniper's features. The thing that troubled the Executioner was that he could easily picture the woman there.

"YOU SHOULD HAVE KNOWN he would wear a bulletproof vest," Norbert Meineck grumbled.

"It was a mistake," Felix Scharnhorst said as he guided the Mercedes to a stop. He'd tuned out the man's whining some time ago. At the bottom of the gentle slope coasting away from the road, the Havel River gleamed under the afternoon sun. "I don't make many mistakes." He set the parking brake, tossed the keys up under the seat and shoved the silenced H&K P-9S into shoulder leather as he got out.

Meineck followed suit, flexing his hands into tight-fitting gloves. "Well, I think you are making another mistake here, my friend. There is no reason to kill this Russian so quickly."

"He can identify us. He and the other one. Possibly the American, as well."

"Scharnhorst, perhaps I need to remind you that most of the members of the RPT are known to the authorities in one way or another. Many of them we culled directly from the ranks of the Red Army Faction. There is no secrecy here save what we rob from the espionage agents."

"And perhaps I need to remind you," Scharnhorst said in an edged voice, "there might come a time when all of us might wish to reenter society with none the wiser."

"By that time, when the wounds between East and West Germany have healed, we will be hailed as heroes. Without interference from the superpowers, we will be well on our way to a new greatness."

Scharnhorst touched the silenced weapon under his coat, then pulled his beret a little lower over his eyes. He smiled to himself as he thought about the events about to transpire.

"I am not the only member of the RPT who faults you for your near miss this morning," Meineck commented.

"I know." It was true. But Scharnhorst was of the opinion that not nearly so much fault would be found without Meineck leading the charge.

"You gave us a great coup when you exposed Karlsruhe as a connection for the United States government," Meineck said. "None of us were aware of that."

"Yes."

"But to miss the shot this morning so badly..." Meineck shook his head.

"Quiet," Scharnhorst warned. "There is our target now." He centered his gaze on the approaching jogger in crimson. Leaning into his steps, he walked down the hill and came to a stop beside the boating dock nearest the jogging trail well ahead of the runner. "Do not look at him."

Meineck joined him at the fence, clinging to mesh wire as if interested only in the armada of sailboats spread out before them.

Scanning the area unobtrusively, Scharnhorst made sure no one paid any undue attention to them. The closest observers were a young mother and her toddler throwing bread crusts to a dozen quacking ducks. He placed his hand around the butt of the pistol and waited. The spare silencer was a comfortable weight in his coat pocket.

He listened as Vasily Starye's footsteps drummed into his ears. Starye was the younger of the two-man team that had been at Restaurant Moskau. Yegor Paputin still remained, but his time of execution was near.

The CIA files on Starye had revealed the young agent's penchant for afternoon jogging near the Havel. As an Intelligence agent, Starye had a lot to learn about maintaining a flexible schedule.

Scharnhorst knew the man would never get the opportunity. He turned as the footsteps rang against the cold concrete and Starye's rhythmic breathing roared into his ears. The 9 mm pistol coughed, and a ragged ribbon chewed across Starye's chest. The Russian went down without a sound.

Kneeling quickly, Scharnhorst leathered his weapon and took the Walther TPH double-action pistol from Starye's ankle holster. It had also been revealed in the CIA files. Chambered for .22LR, the small pistol was an ideal backup piece.

"For God's sake," Meineck said in obvious agitation, "let us get out of here before we are seen." He glanced frantically in all directions.

Working methodically and swiftly, Scharnhorst threaded the extra silencer from his pocket onto the Walther. By the time Meineck looked back at him, he had the deadly little .22 ready to fire. Before the man could speak, Scharnhorst emptied the Walther in a series of miniature pops, scattering the .22 rounds across Meineck's lower face and throat.

The man sagged against the fence, clawing out the final futile seconds of his life.

Unscrewing the silencer from the Walther, Scharnhorst dropped it back in his pocket, then pitched the H&K 9 mm near Meineck. He removed the spare pistol from his coat pocket and leathered it.

No one had noticed anything out of the ordinary yet. The car was registered to Meineck. The pistol was clean. It would look as if Starye and Meineck had killed each other.

Scharnhorst smiled as he walked away. Two more obstacles had been efficiently and successfully eliminated. He was whistling by the time he hit the wooded area and the first scream of discovery ripped through the crisp air.

"THE CIA OFFERED ME sixty thousand dollars to take you down. Even gave me twenty-five thousand of it up front. For expenses, I suppose."

Mack Bolan looked at Firenze Falkenhayn, saw only the dark reflection of his features in her black sunglasses above the cool alabaster of her face. "You do come to the point, don't you?"

"When I think it's necessary."

They sat fogging up the windows of his rented BMW in front of a deserted open-air café in downtown Munich off Thalkirchnerstrasse near Sendlinger Tor Platz. She'd contacted him almost twenty minutes earlier by car phone and set up the meet without saying what it was about. She didn't say how she'd got the number, but the car and the mobile phone had been logged in with the CIA team. Her knowledge lent credence to her Agency ties.

"Why tell me?"

She gave him a small smile. "Don't fool yourself, McKay. Part of me likes you and I respond to that, but I've never let my emotions be my sole guide when I'm out in the field."

"You're curious about the motives behind the order," he said. His own mind was already racing, connecting possibilities, but nothing made sense yet.

"My contacts within the American group are tenuous at best. I never take on anything for them when I can't see both sides of the play."

"You figured if you bounced it off me, you might gain a new perspective on it."

"Yes."

He had to laugh, and it was genuine despite the tension between them. "I can't blame you."

"It's something you would have done had the roles been reversed."

"Yeah."

She removed her sunglasses and studied him with those changing gray eyes. "You're something of a free agent in this thing yourself. Otherwise the CIA wouldn't think they have to fear you."

"Maybe it's not the CIA," Bolan suggested.

She shrugged.

"Who hired you?"

"Even if I told you, you might not believe me. At this very moment you could be thinking this whole thing is nothing more than a fabrication on my part."

"I can check it out. I don't depend on the Agency for my resources."

"And what would that gain us?"

"Maybe a stronger mutual ground."

"A partnership?"

"Something like that."

"Partners from different governments aren't very long-lived in this business." She'd tried to make her tone light, but Bolan heard the bitterness in her voice.

"I'll settle for a truce until we see how this thing shakes down and where all the lines are drawn."

"At this point it sounds like I'm the only one with anything to offer."

"Not true. I know you're a mole for the East German espionage group and you're still in the field."

She looked at him, her face granite hard. She slid the sunglasses back into place and created an effect of greater distance between them.

"You have very good sources," she said.

"They're getting better."

"I don't like having a sword hanging over my head."

"I don't get the impression it's the only one."

She pulled her small pistol from her purse and kept it in her lap as she pointed it at him. "And if I chose to kill you instead?"

"You'd be making the wrong call. I think you know that. My interest here is to find out who's stirring up all the confusion with the assassinations and neutralize them. I believe that pretty much covers the basics of your mission for the East Germans, as well."

"You're very sure of yourself."

"I have to be. You don't have time to second-guess yourself in a hot zone once you've made a decision."

She flicked the safety on the small gun and put it away.

"And I didn't come empty-handed," Bolan said. "I've got a face for the sniper who made the attempt on Karlsruhe today. I also made him as a leader for the RPT who took down Ascherfeld last night."

She wrinkled her brow as she considered that. "You believe there's a connection between the assassinations of foreign agents within the Germanys and the businessmen?"

"This guy's the linchpin."

"Who is he?"

"I don't know. Yet. His picture's on the dash."

Falkenhayn settled back in her seat with the manila envelope.

Bolan watched for a reaction as she slipped the 8 × 10 out and studied it. She didn't flicker an eyelid.

"I don't know him," she said as she tucked the picture back inside the envelope. "May I keep this?"

"Get back to me if you find out something?"

"I can't make any promises. Can you?"

"No."

"Scott hired me to kill you." She arched an eyebrow above the sunglasses. "I might not have been the only one he talked to. Keep that in mind."

"I will."

"You'll be undefensible if you stay with Karl-sruhe's retinue."

"I won't be going back there. I've got some things working that should realign the focus of my mission."

"I cleared my things out after the shooting." She opened the car door and got out, pausing to stick her head back inside long enough to say, "If it means anything, I'm glad I don't have to kill you yet." She shut the door without waiting for his reply.

The Executioner watched her walk away as he keyed the ignition. He flowed into the light traffic as she got into her car, then took his hand from his jacket pocket and placed the .45 in shoulder leather. "Me, too," he said to her reflection in the rearview mirror.

"MY COVER HAS BEEN BLOWN," Firenze Falkenhayn said into the receiver. She stood at a pay phone on Bayerstrasse across from the Rodenstock shop selling binoculars and hunting scopes. She hadn't realized where she had stopped until now, concentrating on making sure she wasn't followed. Thoughts of the sniper scopes available inside the store made the back of her neck itch unpleasantly. She stood with her back pressed to the wall behind her.

"The French?" Rudolph Perbandt asked.

As usual, her East German contact sounded unsurprised.

"No. The American."

"McKay."

"Yes."

"And what does he presume to do with this knowledge?"

"For the moment, nothing."

"So it is to be a bargaining chip?"

She hesitated, then decided to go with certainties rather than feelings. "I don't know."

"This man is growing increasingly dangerous to our efforts," Perbandt said.

Falkenhayn kept her own counsel.

"Have you uncovered his real name?" Perbandt asked.

"No."

Puffing noises came over the receiver as the man stoked his pipe to contemplative life. "He is not coordinating his efforts through the American CIA."

"No." Falkenhayn wondered how he knew. But she was used to Perbandt having access to all kinds of information she was not privy to. "In fact, Scott offered to pay me to kill McKay after the botched attempt on Karlsruhe's life today."

"And?"

"For the moment I thought it more beneficial to leave everything in place."

"Why?"

The suddenness of the question startled her. "I think Scott is acting on his own initiative in this matter. With McKay still alive and making moves of his own, it might create further pressure on whatever organization is moving behind the scenes around us. McKay has already found a connection between the Reunification Party Torch and the group killing German businessmen."

"Do you have proof of this yourself?"

"No." She felt as though she'd unwittingly ventured out onto thin ice.

"So possibly he is leading you on, selling you a bill of goods that will keep you out of his way."

"I had considered that," she said in her own defense.

"You should have listened to your own better judgment," Perbandt chided. "Let me tell you something I think might influence your perspective. McKay's information has come to you through the Russians. Through Paputin."

She knew he paused for her benefit, letting her know he was aware of the light contact she maintained with Paputin.

"McKay has a meeting with Paputin this evening. I think it would be in your interests to be there when they talk." Perbandt gave her the address of the restaurant in West Berlin and the time of the meeting. "I've already arranged for air transportation for you into the city."

"And the French? How am I to explain my sudden absence?"

"Let them stew in their own juices for a while. After this mission is closed down, the decision has been made to bring you in. Once the reunification efforts are more on course, nothing may disturb them."

"Thank you, Rudolph."

"Do not thank me. It has been through your own good work this is happening. Terminate McKay as soon as you are able so we can end this confusion. And take care to come home to us whole." Perbandt broke the connection.

Falkenhayn hung up the receiver and felt the warm tears against her cheeks, cooled quickly by the wind. Her freedom from the lies and counterlies was so near she couldn't believe it. All she had hoped for during these past years. But it would cost the life of another. She squared her shoulders and started for her car.

"PLEASE," Yegor Paputin said as he waved to a dining chair. "Have a seat."

Bolan seated himself at the small linen-covered dining table. The silverware was in neat rolls to the side. Shadows from the trio of tapered candles in the centerpiece wavered across the Russian's face.

"May I pour you a glass of wine, sir?" a waiter asked as he approached their table.

"Just coffee, thanks," Bolan said. Like the Russian, the Executioner wore a black suit that hid the shoulder harness.

The waiter poured, then vanished.

"I took the liberty of ordering ahead," Paputin said.

"I'm not here for the cuisine or the atmosphere."

Paputin sipped his wine, his bald pate gleaming under the subdued lighting. He looked like a gnarled little gnome in a suit too big for him. Then the deadly glitter trapped in his flat black eyes erased the impression. "I understand perfectly, Mr. McKay. Do not underestimate my seriousness about this business. I have been involved in it a long time. I know how seldom a field agent gets to enjoy a hot meal when he is this close to the end of the chase."

"I stand corrected."

"Thank you."

"You think the situation is that close?"

"Most certainly. I can almost see a movie director waiting in the wings to yell 'It's a wrap.'"

Bolan smiled slightly, then leaned back as the waiter returned bearing a tray of food. He spread it out with spectacular efficiency.

"Roast goose," Paputin announced, "and potato dumplings. They cook it with fried fruit in a special gravy. Very filling. Trust me."

The warrior leaned into his portions with gusto. "How far back are your people going to pull you?"

"Much too far to be of any aid during the covert mission. That is why my department was ordered to cooperate with American Intelligence. Our position on this has been compromised. But we may be of assistance once the operation has been exposed for what it is."

"You sound like you know what it is."

"No." Paputin chewed thoughtfully. "We do not know what the final stakes are. But we are certain of some of the players."

"Falkenhayn?"

"She is being used."

"She *is* an East German spy?"

"Of course. We would not offer you false information. At this point, the Germanys are more than willing to view Russia as an oppressor. We join with you to dispute that."

"And the French don't know that she's a plant?"

"Did you?"

"No."

"You must understand something here, Mr. McKay. Everything you see before you was carefully contrived. It was choreographed by an expert many months before these events started to unfold."

"You know the terminations by the Reunification Party Torch and those of the German businessmen are related?"

"Yes. But only for a matter of hours. Though we do not know in what way. Some of the operation's details have begun to leak to East German sources that remain loyal to my country."

Bolan reached under the table and removed a manila envelope from his briefcase containing one of the copies of the sniper. "The man who tried to snuff Karlsruhe today at Oktoberfest."

"As well as the man from Restaurant Moskau last night." Paputin glanced at him. "Do you mind if I keep this?"

"No. Maybe you can turn up something at your end that I can't."

Paputin put the photograph in the seat next to him. "When we know, you will know."

"Fine. Getting back to Falkenhayn."

"Of course. Her control through the East Germans is a man named Rudolph Perbandt. We believe Perbandt is mixed up in the the subterfuge. On the wrong side."

"Professional reasons," Bolan asked, "or personal?"

"Personal. We have the impression there are a lot of capital gains to be made here. But we are unsure how."

Bolan reflected on Ascherfeld's murder briefly and silently agreed. He finished his meal and pushed his plate away. The waiter cleared the dishes and poured coffee refills.

"Falkenhayn is a very good agent," Paputin said. "But you knew that. She would have to be to turn double agent for as many people as she has."

"And Perbandt is using her?"

"Yes. He guided her career through the French espionage units, and managed to supplement her education with his own teachings. Firenze believes implicitly in Perbandt."

"You know her."

"I do. But that does not mean I protect her."

Bolan considered that.

"Ah," Paputin said, "we are about to have company. Were you expecting anyone?"

Bolan glanced over his shoulder and saw Firenze Falkenhayn walking through the dinner crowd. She had changed clothes, opting for evening wear that emphasized her feminine charms. "No, I wasn't."

"This is Perbandt's doing," Paputin said as he got to his feet with a smile on his face that didn't reach his eyes.

"I see," Bolan said. He forced a smile as he wondered if he and the woman were destined to cross swords in this engagement after all.

Paputin must have sensed what was on his mind. "Politics, if served properly, will make enemies of us all."

"FATHER?"

Jeorge Karlsruhe turned from his bedroom window overlooking the rear grounds of the mansion. He put an arm across his chest as he leaned on the cane. Despite the Kevlar vest, the additional padding and the reduced powder powering the bullet, his ribs had been bruised terribly. The pain pills made his head swim. "What is it, Wilhelm?"

"Should you be up? I thought the doctors suggested you stay in bed."

Forcing his shoulders back, Karlsruhe came ramrod erect. "Pah! Doctors don't know everything, Wilhelm." He glanced at the computer disks in his son's hand and resisted the instant flare of anger that filled him. "What is on your mind?"

"Am I disturbing your rest?"

Karlsruhe didn't point out the obvious. "No."

Wilhelm's fingers drummed nervously on the disk container. "I was looking over our finances to figure a way to purchase the new equipment we need to raise our production percentages to rival the Japanese steel manufacturers." He shook his head in perplexion. "Instead, what I found in our portfolio only distressed me further."

Karlsruhe waved toward the small office setup that filled one corner of the huge bedroom. The gleaming metal and squared-off corners of the desk, chairs and filing cabinet contrasted sharply with the baroque style of the bedroom furniture. "You discovered that we have very little in the way of liquid assets at the moment."

Wilhelm sat. His hand strayed to adjust his glasses, just as Karlsruhe knew it would. "Yes."

"And this worries you?"

"Of course, Father, we—"

"Wrong." Karlsruhe's voice was mild rolling thunder. "*I*, Wilhelm, *I*. It has been my hand at the helm of this family's business for a number of years. I have not said I was relinquishing control. Nor have I taken leave of my senses."

"But the investments you've made over the past months," Wilhelm protested. "I have never heard of some of these corporate names."

"Nor were you intended to. You invaded my personal files when you dug out those disks. You had no business doing that."

"I am sorry."

Karlsruhe leaned back in his chair painfully, his hands crossed atop the hawk-headed cane. He let out his breath in a long slow hiss, signaling his contempt. "Those investments are made wisely."

"But many of them are in East German companies."

"Yes."

"Companies we can never hope to be more than merely a minor part of."

"And you think this is bad?"

"Of course I do. If you had come to me with these ideas, I would never have—"

"'Let me,' Wilhelm?"

His son shut up, realizing the mistake he'd almost made.

"There will come a day," Karlsruhe said, "when you will see the wisdom in the things I have done. On that day you will see how I have invested in a united Germany that is going to tear itself free of the husks of the other two. Until then, you will content yourself with supervising the steel mills."

"Yes, Father."

"Leave me. I wish to be alone."

Wilhelm nodded contritely and left the room without another word.

Tapping his cane against the polished wood floor, Karlsruhe peered through the window as one of the helicopters took off. His eyes followed it for a moment as he reflected on the gambles he'd made and the chances he'd taken. It was all worth it, yes. But whether they would pay off was another matter entirely.

The phone rang and he picked it up. "Yes."

"They have agreed to meet," the familiar voice said.

"Where?" Karlsruhe felt his heart pounding against his bruised ribs.

"Tomorrow night. At the Leipzig Fair."

"You will be there, as well?"

"Yes."

"I will see you then." Karlsruhe hung up and smiled. All thoughts of pain were washed away by the promise of successes looming before him.

BOLAN SENSED THE MAN along his backtrail before he saw him. The night had turned dark and ugly while he'd dined with Paputin and Falkenhayn. Conversation had been as light and empty as a confectioner's best efforts. Everyone knew what the other was doing there, but no one said anything about it. Falkenhayn had joined them for dessert, for after-dinner coffee, then they'd broken up. Falkenhayn went off with Paputin. The Executioner recognized it as a weak ploy to make him uncertain of the Russian involvement.

Now, with the wind blowing edged and cold in front of him and the guy on his heels breathing hot and heavy down the back of his neck, the warrior wasn't so sure.

Targeting a nearby van in the crowded parking area beside the restaurant, Bolan turned sharply and disappeared into the shadows surrounding it. Knowing the man would be expecting him to lie in wait, he sprinted instead, circling the van's nose as he drew a silenced SIG-Sauer. The Desert Eagle and his other armament were in the black Porsche Brognola had requisitioned for him.

He crept toward the rear of the van, turned to face any other threat. With the CIA gunning for him, the RPT on the trail of any and all foreign agents, the man who'd linked the RPT with the businessmen executions, French involvement and the East Germans, there was no way of knowing who the silent player belonged to.

He listened as the man's footsteps slowed at the rear of the van, then stopped. He recognized the rustle of metal against hard leather. The footsteps went on.

The Executioner came up behind the man without a sound. He reached for the man's shoulder as the guy crept up on the front of the van, intending to take him alive.

"Warner!" The voice whipped out of the night.

The man turned to face Bolan, dragging an H&K MP-5 from beneath the folds of his coat.

Triggering a pair of rounds that crashed through the white rectangle of the man's forehead under the cold moon, Bolan went to ground as bullets from at least two gunners behind him ripped into the van. Bits of the side mirror tinkled to the ground as he rolled under the vehicle, seeking shelter.

10

The Executioner rolled out from under the van, making a left-to-right sweep with his pistol. He pressed himself up with his free hand, automatically logging the different voices. They spoke German, and he recognized many of the words.

A gunner swung into view to his left and destroyed his brief anonymity.

Leveling the 9 mm, Bolan squeezed off three rapid-fire rounds, aiming by instinct. The gunner toppled over, the H&K MP-5 in his hands inscribing a brief flaming arc.

The warrior charged through the parked cars with his pursuers hot on his heels. His mind flipped through the mental maps he'd made of the area. This was no place for a firefight. There were too many people involved, too much chance of discovery and inadvertent interference. This was strictly hit-and-git. But he had trouble figuring who the intended victim truly was. Echoing gunfire from the street let him know the other two hadn't gone unnoticed.

The yammer of a submachine gun rang out behind him, bullets sparking off the fenders of a low-slung sports car. Bolan leaped, managing the slide across the car's hood like a runner stealing second base, then dropped and cut back to his own vehicle.

Switching his gun to his left hand, he opened the Porsche's door and dropped into the bucket seat. Two men had seen him. He emptied the SIG-Sauer as he reached into his jacket for the keys. The engine started smoothly, revving as he accelerated. He slapped the stick into reverse as he placed the empty pistol on his lap.

Rubber shrieked as he sped out into the lane, bullets lighting brief flares when they ricocheted from the Porsche.

Bolan cut the wheel deftly, reaching under the passenger seat for the Uzi. He thumbed down the electric window and laid the snout of the machine pistol across the door. Passing it over to his left hand, he shifted into first as a gunner stepped into the parking lane ahead of him.

The Porsche's windshield starred as the Executioner touched the Uzi's trigger. A short burst of 9 mm parabellums chopped the man down. The rear end of the sports car dug in when he goosed the accelerator. The Porsche fishtailed for a moment, then settled into the pace.

Tires screaming in protest, Bolan guided the car around the U-shape of the parking area. He caught a glimpse of another gunner coming hard on his right. Knowing the guy was lining him up in the sights of the H&K MP-5, the warrior dropped the Uzi between the seat and the door. He geared down, throwing in the clutch and popping it as he accelerated. The rear of the German sportster came around, losing traction, striking his attacker like a battering ram.

The guy bounced like a rubber ball from the wall behind him, then dropped to the concrete.

Hitting the street in a sideways glide, Bolan shifted up and pulled the sports car back into line. He visually tracked the battlefield.

Falkenhayn was holed up between a line of parked cars and the front of the restaurant. She hovered over Paputin's body with a large pistol clasped in both hands. Two bodies were on the walkway behind her.

Concentrating on the four gunners across the street, Bolan shifted again, gaining speed. He pulled off the street, avoiding the line of parked cars, taking the sidewalk. He hit the lights to gain the attention of the attackers. The nose of the Porsche flattened a slender wrought-iron fence surrounding an empty outside café area. Chairs and small round tables rebounded like tenpins as the car tore through.

The assassins had taken flimsy cover behind the parked vehicles and patio furniture. In one stroke the Executioner rendered them vulnerable, taking away their shelter.

One of them spun around, going down under Falkenhayn's markmanship.

The body thumped under the Porsche's wheels as Bolan cut a swath through them. He clipped one of the retreating men with a fender, then steered back onto the street.

He whipped the rear of the sports car around, tapped the brake firmly and briefly, and pulled a one-eighty as he dropped the transmission into first. The tires smoked when he accelerated, then smoked again as he braked hard and stopped in front of Falkenhayn's position.

Reaching across the seat, he opened the passenger door and said, "Get in." He smashed the dome light as the woman scrambled inside. The brief flicker shone down over Paputin's face. "What about Paputin?"

Falkenhayn shook her head as she loaded a fresh clip into her pistol. "Dead. They killed him."

Bolan powered out onto the street. Bullets smashed against the rear section of the Porsche. Falkenhayn returned fire as rapidly as she could squeeze off the rounds. The sound was thunder inside the car. Hot brass touched Bolan's cheek twice.

He gave himself over to the car as he cut through the traffic. When he saw the sedan cut in front of him, taking up space between the two inner lanes, he knew the team hadn't come alone.

"Company," he said.

Falkenhayn turned her attention from the rear of the car.

Bolan passed over the Uzi, then tapped the glove compartment so it would flip open, revealing the magazines.

The sedan slowed, red lights flaring as the driver stood on the brakes.

Blocked by traffic continuing to pass in both directions on either side of him, the Executioner braked to a halt and put the transmission in reverse. A shot ripped through the windshield, spilling the rearview mirror into the seat beside him. "The tires," he said to Falkenhayn as he sped backwards, holding to his left to dodge traffic that was suddenly oncoming.

The woman leaned out the window and shot out the sedan's rear tires with two quick bursts. Bolan watched

as it spun out of control and got caught up in a collision between two other cars.

Still in reverse, the Executioner shot through a gap
and got onto a side street, bringing the nose of the
Porsche around in a bootlegger's U-turn. He passed
his empty pistol over as he accelerated. After Falkenhayn reloaded, he put it under his thigh for instant
access.

She sat in the passenger seat, breathing hard. A line
of blood smeared her forehead. A quick glance told
Bolan the blood wasn't hers.

She didn't look at him.

Flying through the streets, Bolan used the side mir-
rors to weave a protective visual net around the vehicle. "Did you know them?"

"No." Her voice was flat and undefined.

Bolan glanced at her.

She returned his gaze full measure.

"Do you think they were after Paputin?" he asked.
"Or you?"

"I don't know." She looked forward again. "Yegor went down first."

"They tried to take him that way?"

She shrugged, cold and distant. "Yegor spotted
them. He shoved me out of the way and tried to go for
his gun. Damn fool. He should have taken care of
himself."

Bolan saw a glimmer of tears fill her eyes. She wiped
them away quickly. There wasn't a doubt in his mind
the lady was hanging on to secrets. Whether either of
them survived long enough to unravel them was another matter.

"We need a place to hole up," he said.

"There's nowhere I can go."

"I've got a safehouse. Come with me."

"For now. There is much yet that I must do."

He nodded, then left her with her thoughts as he struggled to sort out his own.

BOLAN STUDIED HER in the darkness from the doorway.

Falkenhayn sat in the large window of the bedroom, chin resting on her knees as she wrapped her arms around her legs. The sun would be up soon, but for now the moon highlighted the unfettered blond hair cascading down her back. She was dressed in a sweatshirt, jeans and joggers. Her pistols, the 9 mm and the .22, lay on the window ledge just behind her feet.

She hadn't said anything during the ride to the safehouse. The conversation after they'd arrived a few hours earlier had been limited to responses to questions concerning comfort and food. There had been no response at all to questions about the hit in front of the restaurant.

He'd had little to say himself. Brognola and Kurtzman had the number to the apartment. Both were supposed to call back as soon as they verified anything.

He listened to the apartment's heater labor to keep up with the demands put on it by the cold weather. Litter in the streets skipped and jumped as the wind ripped at it with unseen talons. The lady appeared as cold as the night. Maybe even as lonely.

Returning to the kitchen, he helped himself to the provisions. The larder was stocked. He took eggs, bell peppers, milk, cheese, ham, butter and jalapeños from the refrigerator. Bread from the small cupboard went for toast. He fried omelets in the biggest skillet he could find, adding the ingredients liberally.

He heated water, figuring Falkenhayn could choose between instant coffee or hot chocolate. He stir-fried chunks of potato in another skillet, got them browned, then put them in a bowl.

She came in as he set the table.

"I never would have thought you were domestic."

"You haven't eaten it yet." Bolan covered the table with the food, finishing with the pot of hot water. He'd showered and shaved, then dressed in jeans and a T-shirt, no shoes, but the shoulder holster was in place.

She sat.

Bolan passed out the utensils and condiments. They ate in silence and, though he'd fixed enough for four people, there was nothing left when they finished.

"Guess I didn't know how hungry I really was," Falkenhayn said as she nursed her second cup of chocolate.

Bolan started to clear the dishes, but she waved him to his seat. He poured himself another cup of coffee and watched her work.

She moved with an economy of motion, fully feminine despite the unseen weapons he knew were there. "Yegor had a wife, you know." She stared at the line of tap water filling one half of the double sink.

"No," Bolan replied. "I didn't."

"Her name is Larochka. They had three children. Two girls and a boy. He was very proud of them."

Bolan said nothing, feeling the maelstrom of emotions swirling within the woman. Things would come out as they were ready. Rushing them would only cause her to retreat into herself again.

"I wonder," Falkenhayn said, turning toward him, "how she'll take it when she's told he's dead. Do you think she'll believe it was worth it? That it was worth her husband dying?"

"I don't know."

She went back to work on the dishes. "I wouldn't, McKay, and that's the hell of it. Caught up as I am in the middle of everything, I can say, yes, I'd die for the cause. Only now, I'm not so sure what the cause is anymore. How much do you know about Yegor and me?"

"Nothing. I was only informed that Paputin was my contact with the Russians."

"Yegor introduced me to this business. He set me up with my current supervisor."

"In the Stasi?"

"Yes. It was KGB-operated in the beginning."

Bolan nodded.

"Yegor met me while I was with GIGN. I was a young girl, filled with passion for a homeland I'd never seen. My father's homeland. My father talked of it often despite the move back to France with my mother, of how the great wound in the Germanys would never heal, of how families would continue to be torn apart by the East and the West. At first I was motivated by his stories, then I adopted his memories as my own. I wanted something better for my country. My father died the year before the Wall went down."

She clenched her fists and pressed them against the countertop. "The hit at the restaurant was an attempt to wipe the slate clean," she said in a harsh voice.

"Yes."

"You're a recognized threat, McKay."

"I know."

"See? At first I could buy that. I could believe the team had been assigned to assassinate you. Perhaps even Paputin, because relations between the Stasi and the KGB have shattered." She broke off.

"You were set up," Bolan stated. "My sources have confirmed the hit team as East German. Some of them were known Stasi. And that means Perbandt had it in mind for you to get taken down, too."

She looked at him.

"It's true," Bolan said. He leaned forward, placing his elbows on the table. "This doesn't come as any surprise."

"You got this from the phone call earlier?"

The Executioner nodded.

"Why didn't you tell me then?"

"If I had, would you have believed me?"

"I don't know."

"I had to let you work it through for yourself."

"Your caller had no other information to volunteer?"

"No. Intel is lean now, but it's getting ready to break. You stay at this sort of thing long enough, you get to where you can sense it."

"I feel it, too."

Bolan sipped his coffee, waiting.

"I've allowed myself to be blinded."

"Yes." He didn't flinch from the truth. Whatever happened now, they had to have that between them.

She walked away from the sink, arms crossed over her breasts. "So why have you kept me here? You could have easily turned me over to the CIA."

"The CIA team in this sector's been infiltrated," Bolan replied. "Scott's trying to set up that contract on me told me that. And the RPT's had too much information on European and British agents. Once I had Scott in my sights, it wasn't too hard to make the necessary leap in logic to figure he was feeding Intel to the RPT through channels."

She turned back to face him, a dark silhouette against the curtained window. "That still doesn't explain what I'm doing here."

"We're the only two players left in the field who know the terrain," the warrior said. "I'm organizing a surgical strike on this."

"The Russians?"

"At this point they look like the only espionage team we can rely on. If steps are taken to remove Scott from his present position, it's going to send messages to the people behind this. Chances are, even if he would talk and incriminate himself, Scott would be dead before we could get him out of the country. I want them to believe they have everything sewn up."

"What about the West Germans?"

"They may be leaking as badly."

"And me?"

"You're the wild card. You have information that can be used against whoever's putting this together. You have insights that can give us a bigger picture."

"That's why you've stayed here? To persuade me to work with you?"

Bolan shook his head. "I can't persuade you. There just hasn't been anything else I could do."

"I could lie."

"Yeah."

"But you don't think I would."

"Sure. If the motivations were right. So would I. I believe they aren't. If I'm right about what's going down on this thing, there's a lot to lose if the final play isn't exactly right."

"Nothing can stop the reunification."

"No, but it sure as hell can be set back years if not decades. Things haven't been easy. They can be made worse."

"What do you have in mind?"

"You and I are going to run point on this operation. When the time is right, we're going to blow the whistle on the people behind this and kick their damn house down."

"How do you know you can trust me?"

Bolan returned her gaze full measure. "I see a lot of myself in you. You're tough, aggressive, and you've had no choice but to go independent for a long time. You want to believe in ideals. I've weathered some tough storms myself. You won't let this break your beliefs or stop you from wanting them. By staying hard and standing on your own, you've learned to make your own decisions and to trust your own judgment."

Her voice was strained when she spoke a few seconds later. "You're quite the philosopher."

"I don't mean to be. You wanted to know what was on my mind. I told you. The rest is up to you."

"And what do you get out of this?"

"Somebody at my back I don't have to check on when things get dirty."

"Things will."

"I know."

"Perbandt will know I'm on to him."

"I'm counting on that. It'll provide some additional worrying that may create stress cracks we can use."

"But what is this all about?"

Bolan showed her a mirthless grin. "It's an old song. You should recognize it without the words. Power and money."

"But how?"

"I'm not sure yet. But I *am* sure it's there. I got the scent of it when Ascherfeld was killed. The man had salted away millions during his tenure in the East German government. Those millions haven't turned up, so I'm assuming they were what the killers were after."

"So where does he fit?"

"Right now I only know Ascherfeld fits because he *doesn't* fit. The RPT is in bed with the same people who've killed German businessmen working for reunification. I ID'ed the shooter who attempted the takeout on Karlsruhe, and I saw him before the night Ascherfeld was killed. The CIA section chief in the area has been bought off. The same can be said of Stasi members."

"If it boils down to money, they're going to need somebody who can assimilate and disperse large amounts of cash."

Bolan noted the blaze of excitement in the woman's eyes. "That's what I'm thinking."

"There's one name that immediately comes to mind."

Nodding, Bolan said, "Jeorg Karlsruhe."

WAKING FROM the light doze he'd allowed himself to fall into on the couch, Bolan answered the phone on the second ring.

"We ID'ed your face," Aaron Kurtzman said.

Bolan sat up, rubbing his face with a hand. Bright sunlight stabbed in through the apartment's windows. He adjusted the shoulder holster in an attempt to restart circulation. "Who is he?"

"Felix Scharnhorst. He was a member of the Munich police department for eight years. Two years ago he resigned and sought private employ as a security guard. Want to make a guess who he went to work for?"

"Jeorg Karlsruhe."

"I don't have a bell, Striker, or I'd be ringing the hell out of it right now. You don't sound surprised."

"I've been looking in Karlsruhe's direction for a while now."

"Yeah, well, Karlsruhe's still got his aces wired as far as the State Department and the Pres are concerned."

"So we'll wake them up when the time's right."

"And that's not now?"

"Not until I get a handle on Karlsruhe's plans."

"Maybe I can shed some light in that direction, too."

"The money surfaced?"

"Ascherfeld's, yeah. Tracing back through electronic transfer records, I found out Ascherfeld's secret accounts were siphoned off within an hour of his death."

"Dead men tell no tales."

"You figure Ascherfeld as an operator on this?"

"No," Bolan replied, "I figure Ascherfeld was fingered for the money. So where is it now?"

"Being plowed back into the East German economy through an aggressive stock market firm secretly controlled by Jeorg Karlsruhe. The company's mortgaged everything they could get their hands on to buy as much East German company stock as they've been able. And get this—that same company's holding some stock under an alias I've identified as belonging to CIA section chief John Scott."

"We know Scott's in it."

"Up to his eyeballs."

Bolan registered that, trying to work through it. "Lay it out for me, Aaron. Brokering was never one of my favorite subjects. If the money's being plowed back into the East German economy, how's that hurting anything? Except Ascherfeld."

"It's the way it's being put in. This firm is working through dozens of dummy corporations. The East Germans are hurting. They can't compete with the West German market without getting some investment capital to upscale their equipment. With the Wall gone, East German consumers are going into West Germany to buy goods."

"Leaving East German competitors out in the cold."

"Exactly. So they put shares of their company up for sale, trying to squirrel enough back so no one can get a majority against the owners. Problem is, in order to raise the necessary capital, they've had to turn loose a lot of shares. The stock market firm has been quietly funneling them into one pocket."

"Giving the owner the majority of the stock in a lot of businesses for dirt-cheap prices."

"For a layman you're not so bad."

"I learned from the Mafia, Aaron. Best organized criminal system in the world during their time."

"Yeah, but you ought to see the details on insider trading one of these days."

Bolan stood, carrying the phone to the dining table. He put water on for coffee. "I'll need hard copy on this."

"It'll be faxed wherever you want it as soon as you give the word. You're going to have to take the operation down quick. Otherwise the stock market firm will melt away without even leaving a bathtub ring."

"No evidence freezes us out, too."

"Yeah. And doesn't do squat about kissing the relationships between the U.S. and Germany and making them better. This has been put together well, Striker. If I hadn't been tipped about Ascherfeld's money, I wouldn't have found it at all."

"I'll be in touch. And thanks, guy."

"No prob."

Bolan broke the connection and punched Brognola's number. A male voice took a message after saying Brognola was out. He called Karlsruhe's mansion and talked with Peg Morelund, finding out Karlsruhe had left earlier. There had been no word where the man was going or when he would be back.

He glanced at his watch, found out it was after 2:00 p.m. and later than he'd thought. If anything had broken he should have known about, Brognola would have called.

Now, with the clock ticking and the last handful of numbers trickling into play, he was restless and edgy. Still barefoot, he padded through the bedroom and into the bathroom.

Falkenhayn lay wrapped up in the sheets and blanket on the bed. Hard-edged metal gleamed under her pillow.

He shaved and took another shower. Steam covered the window as he redressed and examined his neck. Angry red colored the edges, showing the infection trying to gain a foothold.

"Let me."

Bolan glanced up, seeing Falkenhayn's face in the mirror space he'd cleared with a swipe of his hand. "Thanks." He passed over the first-aid kit. With the smallness of the room and only the towel around his waist, he was extremely conscious of the woman standing so near him.

She wore a long-sleeved man's shirt. Nothing else. The shirttails barely covered her haunches. She looked up at him as she put the bandage in place. When she was finished, she placed a hand on his chest, bare and electric. "There's more between us than just a trust, isn't there?"

"Maybe," he admitted.

"I felt it from the very first time I saw you." She smiled and shook her head. "'Kindred spirits' is something you'd expect to find in a romance novel."

"Unless you happen to believe in them."

She touched his face with her fingers, exploring the uneven planes of his features. "I'm scared, McKay."

"It's okay to be scared."

"Are you?"

"Yes."

"I don't want to die."

He closed a gentle hand around her fingers. "Nobody does."

"I've never been this far over the edge, never been this far away from everything I know."

"You mean everything you thought you knew. You've been in free-fall for a long time. The thing you need to remember is that you've survived there by yourself."

"Is that what keeps you going?"

"Sometimes."

"And after this?"

"There's another war to be fought somewhere else."

She shook her head. "I don't want that for me."

"Then don't accept it."

"It's not that easy."

"No. It's that hard."

"Are you being a philosopher again?"

He smiled. "No. I've been on this road a long time."

"Too long to get off?"

"Yes."

"I see so much life in you. How can you accept death?"

"I'm not accepting it. I'm fighting it every step of the way."

"I heard the phone call. Is it time to go?"

"Not yet."

"But soon?"

"Yes."

Her eyes searched his. "Do I have to ask?"

"No." Bolan reached down and pulled her into his arms. Her mouth fastened to his as he carried her to the bed. Somewhere in there the shirt and towel disappeared. He felt her need to be secure in the middle of all the fear, and he responded to it by giving in to his own desires. Both of them were fired by a primeval urge to survive, and there was the subconscious affinity for each other. The chemistry was right, but there would never be a right time.

He covered her body with his, amazed at the mixture of hardness and softness. They found a rhythm that seemed natural, that threatened to sweep their breath away, that poised them on the bittersweet edge of existence and spoke of sharing.

It was a reaching out, an exploration of feelings that could never be released between them again. Balanced on the edge of life and death, Bolan found the essence of himself and surrendered to the answering spark inside the woman. Her breath was soft in his ear, quietly urging him on.

"STRIKER?"

Bolan held the receiver to his ear as he sat up in bed. Falkenhayn rolled off him and watched his eyes. "Yeah."

"I got a note that said you called," Brognola said.

"I need to know where Karlsruhe is." He glanced at his watch. It was 3:45 p.m.

"Leipzig Fair," the head Fed replied. "There was a special meeting put together by the East German businessmen to discuss reunification plans. They're knuckling under to the 'outside interference' bullshit. Even Karlsruhe's selling that now."

"I'm not surprised," Bolan said. "It's all working out to his benefit. I don't have time to go into it. Check in with the Bear for the details. In the meantime get those raiding parties of yours on the alert."

"That is it?"

"Yeah. One way or the other." Bolan hung up, then looked at Firenze. "We're on."

11

Leipzig Fair was in full swing when Bolan and Falkenhayn arrived. Tents and permanent buildings dotted the rolling landscape. Brightly lighted carnival rides whirled up and down or around and around. A cacophony of voices shadowed with adult enthusiasms and the excited shrieks of children created an audio fallout.

Bolan left the car in the thick mud covering the temporary parking area, then headed toward the fairgrounds. He wore the skintight blacksuit under a dark trench coat. A watch cap covered his head and the tips of his ears. The Desert Eagle rode his hip, and a SIG-Sauer was snugged in shoulder leather. He had a H&K 94 A-3 semiautomatic carbine slung over his shoulder under the coat. Extra magazines for all his weapons hung from his combat harness, as did a small selection of grenades.

Falkenhayn was a silent wraith at his side. She wore a smaller version of the blacksuit under her long coat. Her blond hair was pinned up under a dark beret. Her rigging was similar to his. Her 9 mm pistol rode in a belly holster, while the .22 hung in breakaway leather under her arm. Instead of a carbine, she'd opted for an Uzi machine pistol.

He paid their entrance fee, and they stepped into the kaleidoscopic effect of the fair. Music blared from horns, mixing in with the broadcast voices announcing different contests and shows.

The Executioner scanned the crowds. Identification would be hard except for the key players. There was no way of knowing how many men Perbandt might have infused through the Stasi. Karlsruhe's own resources seemed endless. Then there was the question of how deeply Scott had allowed treachery to seep into the ranks of the CIA.

They passed the amusement rides, working a spiral that churned them into the guts of the fair. Strings of electric lanterns hung along the walkways. The illumination was faint and uncertain.

Ten minutes later Bolan made the first perimeter guard. He waved Falkenhayn into the shadow of a tent. "Do you see him?" he asked.

She glanced over his shoulder, then gave a short, quick nod. "One of Perbandt's men."

He slipped the SIG-Sauer from shoulder leather and concealed it in the pocket of the trench coat. Guiding her away from the guard, he heard the numbers starting to fall in his head.

They passed three more guards before he found Karlsruhe's chauffeur leaning against a luxury rental car sitting with a half-dozen others a short distance from a two-story building.

"Scott," Bolan said, nodding toward the man leaving the building.

"Evidently he didn't stay in Berlin."

Bolan melted within the shadows as he followed along the rogue CIA agent's trail.

Scott walked into a public rest room in one of the permanent buildings across from an open tent showcasing wooden handicrafts.

The Executioner stepped inside after the man, blinking against the sudden brightness of the light. A peal of thunder ricocheted from outside. Three other men were in the rest room. He brushed by them, aiming for the metal stall Scott was sliding into.

The CIA man's eyes widened as he saw Bolan. A hand dipped under his jacket.

The warrior didn't hesitate. He lifted a booted foot and smashed it into the stall door. The impact knocked Scott backward, dropping him into the porcelain toilet bowl. Then he showed the man the business end of the SIG-Sauer. "It's your call," the Executioner growled, "and I got the only ace showing."

Scott slumped into the bowl, his shoulders resting against the wall behind him as he held up his hands. A crimson trickle of blood ran down his chin from the corner of his mouth.

Stepping forward, Bolan reached for the exposed butt of the CIA agent's pistol. Scott made a last desperate play, kicking out with his foot and going for the gun again. Reacting instantly, the warrior deflected the kick with his thigh, then backhanded the agent and thumped the man's head off the cinder-block wall. He had no trouble getting the gun and pocketing it.

He grabbed the collar of Scott's coat and yanked the man to his feet. The brief scuffle had attracted the attention of the other people in the rest room. Bolan smiled reassuringly at them and said in German, "Too much to drink."

Scott stumbled out under his guidance, groaning slightly and bearing out Bolan's words.

"I got a news flash for you, Scott," the Executioner said as they stepped outside. Lightning flashed overhead, followed immediately by another peal of thunder. Light rain dappled the tents. "You're made. The Agency's going to learn before tonight's over how dirty you are. You understand me?"

"Yeah, yeah," Scott said, holding his hands up in front of his face defensively.

"Strike teams are waiting out there right now," Bolan told him. "We know all about Karlsruhe's bid to sweep East German industry through the phoney stock firm. We know he's tied to the Reunification Party Torch and to the assassinations of the East German businessmen who wouldn't play ball with him. We know Scharnhorst faked the attempt on Karlsruhe. Are you following me here?"

Scott nodded.

Falkenhayn stepped from the shadows.

Scott's eyes darted to the woman, then back to Bolan.

"Yeah," the Executioner said, "I know about that little bit of business, too. If you answer my questions, you get a chance to run as far and as fast as you can before I shut Karlsruhe down."

Wiping his mouth with the back of his hand, Scott said, "What do you want to know?"

"Why the meeting tonight?"

"Perbandt set it up," Scott said, glancing at Falkenhayn. "The people gathered there are the ones who've held out the longest before selling their stock. Perbandt convinced them he'd run security on the meeting. Karlsruhe's already worked out deals with their heirs through third parties about purchasing the stock.''

"He's going to kill them?"

"Yeah. Going to give them a stroke speech, then blow up the building."

"How?"

"It's wired, man. I did it myself. The detonation devices and explosives I used are going to point directly to the United States and Russia. That way Karlsruhe gets rid of the last line of resistance and ensures the reunification efforts will be isolated until he can solidify his position."

"Who has the detonator?"

"Karlsruhe."

Blood chilling at the thought of the carnage awaiting release at the heart of the packed fair, Bolan shoved Scott away from him. "Start running," he said in a cold voice. "Don't even stop to look over your shoulder because you might find a bullet waiting there."

Scott stumbled away, forcing himself into a ragged run that lost him inside the crowd.

Bolan turned back to the meeting place, taking long strides. Falkenhayn matched him, her pistol already bright and hard in her fist. "We won't have time to wait on the strike teams," he said.

"I know."

"If Perbandt or Karlsruhe gets away, everything we've tried to salvage goes down the drain. Without proof, there's no way of clearing this up."

"They won't," she said grimly.

Bolan nodded, then keyed the signaling device in his pocket to summon Brognola's shock troops.

"EVERYTHING GOES as we have expected," Rudolph Perbandt said. In his early sixties the Stasi agent maintained himself through proper diet and exercise. His body was long and lean, sculpted of muscled planes. His shaved head gleamed under the subdued lighting of the meeting room.

Jeorg Karlsruhe would have bet the man's Panzer uniform still fit as well as it had when Perbandt had served in Rommel's Afrika Korps. He reached for the champagne on one of the long banquet tables, then refilled his glass and Perbandt's. "There is no other way things could have gone," Karlsruhe said. "We planned each and every detail, you and I. I look upon our accomplishment as nothing more than a reflection of our combined skills. I was very fortunate to find someone as intelligent as yourself."

"Pah," Perbandt said. "Fortune had nothing to do with it. You sought me out."

"True." Karlsruhe glanced around the large room.

Nearly twenty men, a selection of the cream of East Germany's industrial circles, chatted in groups and picked at the large buffet he had ordered for them. The room was done in a festive fashion, decorated in bright colors with islands of balloons bobbing along the rows of tables.

He ran his thumb along the hard outlines of the electronic device inside his tuxedo pocket and smiled. He glanced up at Perbandt. "Even with these fools out of the way, things will take time to develop."

"But they will develop."

"Yes. Gradually they will learn of the stock options I have purchased, and of the CEO position I have reserved for myself. By then they will still be more afraid of outsiders than they are of me. If any dare protest, you will have your people silence them."

"Yes."

"And the highly touted reunification will build us an empire in what used to be East Germany. Here, where the investment dollar goes farther, where labor prices will not truly affect profits for years, perhaps decades, we will begin new fortunes for ourselves. Even the Japanese manufacturers will learn to fear us."

"Because we will be more palatable to the American and European market than the Orientals." Perbandt smiled. "In the meantime they will blame each other for what has happened here to alienate them from buying into the stock market."

Karlsruhe nodded and raised his champagne glass. "To the future of empires."

"As you will." Perbandt clinked his glass against Karlsruhe's.

Karlsruhe placed his glass on a serving tray one of the black-suited waiters carried. Glancing at the chandelier overhead, he caught a flicker of movement along the second-story balcony that ran around the room. Empty seats ringed the floor.

A shadow separated itself from the hovering darkness encouraged by the selective lighting. Karlsruhe recognized the man at once despite the dark clothing: McKay, the American reporter who was something more and something less than CIA.

Clasping the detonator through the folds of the tuxedo, he brushed by Perbandt, slipping through the crowd toward a nearby doorway.

"What is it?" Perbandt demanded.

"McKay," Karlsruhe said as he jerked his arm free. He got the attention of a security guard. "Up on the second floor. Get the others and kill that damn interferer once and for all."

The man nodded and moved into action.

Perbandt disappeared into the crowd as the sharp crack of gunshots echoed inside the room. Then the American's voice bellowed out for all to hear, telling them that the building had been wired with explosives.

Karlsruhe ran as fast as he could, sucking in great drafts of air as his heart hammered inside his bruised chest. He knocked over plastic plants in his rush toward the back door and his waiting limousine. It could all still be salvaged. He was sure of that. Once he was clear of the area, he would detonate the building and let the Americans and Russians fight each other for the blame. Perhaps it would set him back a few years, but surely he still had those years left.

He pushed through the last door, wheezing and out of breath. The cool air hit him like a physical blow. He loosened his collar, screaming for Isaak to open the limo's door and for Scharnhorst to accompany him. The detonator was a hard rectangle in his hand.

MACK BOLAN FIRED the H&K 94 A-3 with the stock still folded, leaning out over the railing. The harsh crack of the 9 mm rounds reverberated inside the domed roof. He'd shed the trench coat before the brief climb up to the second story from an adjacent building.

He leaned into each shot, absorbing the recoil, ignoring the open sights. There wasn't time for pinpoint accuracy. The drumroll of gunfire answered any questions the people below might have. The 15-round clip emptied as return fire chewed along the wooden railing and whipped by his head.

He dived, pulling a pair of flash grenades from his harness. Yanking the pins as more shooters zeroed in on his position, he tossed the bombs into the open, aiming for the stage below.

Twin thunderclaps rattled the interior of the building as a double flash of lightning cored through the dim light.

Vibrations warned him of the approaching men using the side stairs. He rammed a fresh magazine into the assault rifle and fed in the first round. Flipping the retractable stock out, he locked it into place.

A head showed above the top step of the stairway to his left.

The Executioner sighted briefly, then squeezed the trigger as a muzzle-flash erupted from the guy's pistol. The shooter's bullet lodged into the carpet and wooden floor inches ahead of the warrior. Bolan's round took the man between the eyes and blew him back down the stairway.

Pushing himself to his feet, the Executioner glanced between the planks of the railing and spotted more men wavering undecided on the other stairway. He punched five quick rounds among them, downing at least two of their members and convincing the rest a vertical assault on the second floor wasn't the wisest of moves.

He checked the banquet area. The crowd had evaporated. A tumbled disarray of tables and service trays showed they hadn't been organized about their leaving.

Bolan retreated, dodging back up toward the window he'd used to get inside the building, leaping over rows of seats. He cleared the last row as voices shouted behind him.

"Spread out!" someone yelled in German. "Get the bastard!"

Reflected neon lights of a half-dozen colors speared into the upper balcony from the fair. Even in the darkness filling most of the area, Bolan knew his discovery was only moments away—if the explosion didn't get them all first.

He scanned the walls in desperation as the cautious footsteps closed in on him. When he saw the foam-filled fire extinguisher hanging on a wall twenty feet away, he shouldered the carbine and fired two shots.

White foam erupted from the holed container, spraying wildly. Autofire raked the canister from the wall before someone could gain control of the shooters.

Bolan pushed up and sprinted toward the window. The top of a tent stood out against the black sky. He'd noted it on his climb into the building. He crossed his arms in front of his face and jumped, offering a silent prayer to the universe that he'd make the fifteen feet. Bullets hammered into the walls as the gunners tried too late to track him.

Bolan twisted in midair, heartened immediately when he saw he'd achieved the necessary distance. The canvas material of the tent spread out before him as he angled his fall.

Then the building blew. Fire spread in gouts, like blood running from an open wound. An invisible hand formed of the resulting concussive force slammed into the Executioner, turning the fall all wrong.

FIRENZE FALKENHAYN watched Perbandt as the Stasi commander ran from the building. McKay's shots still rang in her ears, punctuated by the frightened voices echoing in their wake.

For a moment her attention wavered as she saw Karlsruhe crawl into his limousine. Then she clamped her jaw tight.

She pushed thoughts of days and months, and even years, of being lied to from her mind. She had to be focused. Perbandt posed as much of a threat to the success of their mission as Karlsruhe. And for one-on-one, Perbandt was much more dangerous.

Confusion whipped through the fair as people became aware of the military assault going on inside the building. Yelling men spilled from the doors, instantly forming a glut around the parked cars.

She hesitated as Karlsruhe's limo finally freed itself of the snarled knot, throwing streams of muddy clouds from the spinning tires. Aching with the indecision of the moment, she made herself choose. She carried the .22 clenched in her hand as she raced after Perbandt.

Karlsruhe, traveling by the limousine McKay had already seen, would be easy to trail. Perbandt, choosing to make his escape through the crowds, would not.

She raced after him, amazed at the old man's speed. Her booted feet sank in the mud in the narrow alleys between the tents and buildings of the fair. She slipped as she turned a corner by a pastry stand, sliding to one knee in the cold mud. Rain fell in cold, stinging pellets now, savaging her face and making her narrow her eyes.

Perbandt gained a small, precious distance, becoming a dark blot against the blunted yellow lights of the carousel ahead of him.

Falkenhayn rose and stumbled forward, forcing herself into a slogging run. Mud dripped from her hands. She took a firmer grip on the .22.

The explosion erupted behind her. She saw Perbandt turn to survey the damage, coming to a halt, silhouetted against the colorful horses as they bobbed up and down to the blared sound of an East German marching song.

Halting, she brought her pistol up, bracing it against her forearm, centering the sights on Perbandt. She fired twice as the man ducked and fled. Cursing, she pressed on after him. She knew she'd missed. With only thirty feet between them, she'd jerked the trigger instead of squeezing it.

It was the mistake that could be expected of a novice. Now it might be a mistake that not only cost her life, but the lives of several others as the reunification issue turned bloody.

But there was no denying the cold fear that filled her when Perbandt's eyes locked on her. He had known her, had trained her, had been as much a parent to her in his own way as any parent she'd had.

She steeled herself, remembering the lifeblood trickling from Paputin's wounds. The Russian's death rattle would haunt her nights for the rest of her life.

The rain made the ground more slick. She had trouble running, had trouble making the corners as she sped up to cut the distance between herself and Perbandt.

Lights flared at the other end of the aisle as she turned around the corner. A four-wheel-drive jeep bucked through the ruts over a hundred yards away. She saw the armed men inside it as the crowd of people before the vehicle parted and quickly got out of the way.

For a moment Perbandt was bathed in the headlights, then he ducked inside a long, wide tent.

Falkenhayn followed, holding her pistol in both hands. The smell of wet animals and mildewed straw filled her nostrils. The whickerings of horses and lowing of cows echoed around her. She couldn't see in the darkness and went forward slowly. Iron bars closing off the different stalls of the show animals made an unbroken line to the other end of the tent. Two exits were outlined by the outside light. She leveled the .22 in front of her.

"Firenze." Perbandt's voice was soft, filled with the authority that had always been there. "Go away now and you will not be hurt."

She froze and ducked lower, trying to estimate where the words had come from.

"Do not try to hide from me, girl. I know you are there."

"You betrayed me," Falkenhayn said, taking a cautious step. She concentrated on the left. "You betrayed the German people."

"And now I do not deserve to live?"

"You may surrender if you wish. I will accept it."

Perbandt's laughter mocked her words. "You are brash. But you are naive. You allow yourself to be led by your beliefs."

"But not by my emotions," Falkenhayn said. "You drilled that out of me, remember?" She took a step, then another. Horses trotted nervously in their stalls, banging shoed feet against the wooden planks. "Greed is an emotion, Perbandt. One of the seven deadly sins. And you have let it rule your life these past months. Perhaps it has been there for years. Now it has led you here."

"To what?"

Falkenhayn remained silent, took another step.

"My death? Now you are playing the fool. I am your teacher, girl."

"And I learned well. I learned to lie, steal and kill at your bidding. How you must have laughed as you made your plans with Karlsruhe, thinking of the poor deluded girl who lived three lifetimes as your puppet." Falkenhayn continued her slow progress as she passed the halfway point. Tension knotted her stomach, threatened to blur her eyes with tears and cause her hands to shake. She firmed her grip on the pistol. "You tried to make me into a weapon that would serve only you."

"I succeeded."

"No," she said in a harsh voice. "Weapons have no conscience. I do, and I will have no more of your borrowed guilt on my head."

"Is this what you want, Firenze? To die like one of the animals around us? You have no chance against me."

Even as Perbandt's voice died away, the Stasi agent made his move.

Falkenhayn caught the flicker of movement from the corner of her eye and wheeled to counter it. The barrel of the .22 came around, aiming squarely at the moving silhouette. The muzzle-flash formed a yellow-orange cone just before the sledgehammer impact hit her in the arm and toppled her from her feet.

Without trying to rise from the straw-covered ground, knowing she didn't have time for that, she extended her gun arm and emptied the .22's clip at the second muzzle-flash, *squeezing* every shot.

CURLED INTO A BALL, Bolan struck the tent off balance. His weight and the force of his diving fall tore the aluminum frame of the structure loose, allowing the folds of the canvas to wrap around him. His lungs emptied as a pole smashed across his midsection.

Heat spread across the material covering his back, letting him know a sheet of flames had covered the tent. He hung suspended off the ground by the sagging tent as the fire burned holes in the canvas covering the upper section. Forcing his hand through the twisted material, he found the hilt of his Cold Steel Tanto. The blade whisked through the canvas, and he dropped through. Flaming embers rained around him.

He sucked in his first breath and coughed as smoke seared his lungs. His hands darted around his military rigging instinctively, making sure his equipment was still in place. The carbine was gone, lost somewhere in the confusion of the fall.

Drawing the Desert Eagle, he jogged to the front of the tent, taking cover behind the writhing flaps for a moment. He scanned the fair.

Wreckage of the building had been blown in all directions. Scott had been right. It *had* been a good demolition job. The group of cars in front of the building had been literally covered by falling debris. A scattering of fires licked at the stranded vehicles, crawling in through open doors.

The Executioner noticed the absence of Karlsruhe's vehicle at once. He left the tent, scrambling toward the knot of cars with the .44 held low by his leg. Knowing Brognola and his troops would have all the usual exits from the fairgrounds shut down, Bolan ran for the wooded area to the south of the fairgrounds proper.

A study through binoculars from the outer perimeter before they'd arrived had shown Bolan the backtrail that had been made cross-country in drier times. He was sure Karlsruhe would know about it, too. The man possessed an animal cunning and a high regard for the safety of his own hide.

Topping the ridge at the fringe of the fairgrounds, he looked down the incline. Brake lights flared ruby in the distance, perhaps eighty yards away, telling him he'd been right. The car was the same one Karlsruhe's chauffeur had been leaning against earlier.

Bolan ran as the sound of battle filled the area behind him. Autofire rumbled uncertainly, then found renewed life. Sirens screamed.

Breathing through his nose, Bolan concentrated on his stride, forcing as much power into it as he could. He raced down the incline, keeping the heavy .44 tucked in close to his chest.

Karlsruhe's limo wasn't going anywhere. The gunning engine and wet whine of the tires told the warrior it had mired in the muddy field. It rocked steadily, lunging forward then backward as the driver attempted to free it.

The Executioner kept to the shadows, maintaining cover from the surrounding foliage. The broken terrain hampered him only slightly.

When he was less than twenty yards from the stranded limousine, a muzzle-flash flared from his right.

He went to ground as the echoing trio of gunshots rolled over him. He checked his instinctive response to return fire, knowing the muzzle-flash would give away his position. He got to his feet in a crouch.

The limo's transmission continued to groan as it shivered and struggled in the mud. The lunges became longer, signaling the vehicle's impending release. Less than a hundred yards remained between it and the closest street. If the limo reached the pavement, Bolan knew he didn't have a chance of catching it or Karlsruhe.

He circled in the darkness, trying to skyline his attacker against the night sky.

Abruptly the limo broke free, shedding clods of semidry clay as it wheeled out backward. The bright reverse lights played over the foliage, painting it black on white.

After a moment of blindness, Bolan saw Felix Scharnhorst illuminated by the reverse lights. The whitewash faded away as the ruby glow of the taillights flared up again. Spots dancing in front of his eyes, the Executioner lifted the .44 Magnum in a Weaver stance, focusing on Scharnhorst.

Scharnhorst's gun blossomed flame again.

The bullet went wide, then the Desert Eagle chugged in rapid fire in the warrior's hand. Sparks flared from a metal button over Scharnhorst's chest as the heavy slugs kicked the man backward.

Bolan was in motion even as Scharnhorst's corpse toppled to the muddy ground.

The chauffeur stood on the accelerator, bumping along a new course that took the limo around the problem area. The headlight beams bounced crazily.

Driving his feet into the earth, Bolan ran, gaining on the heavy vehicle as it floundered in its efforts to accelerate. He emptied the Desert Eagle's clip into the tires, then recharged the .44 as the metal rims ripped their way into the mud, dropping the limo's carriage to ground level.

Breathing heavily, the Executioner leaned down and opened the back door. He waved the chauffeur and the financier out of the car as a wave of jeeps sporting whirling cherries swept over the incline.

"It's over," Bolan said to Karlsruhe as the jeeps surrounded them. "You know how it is with these hostile takeovers. One day you're on top, then you're history the next. You won't even rate a footnote."

EPILOGUE

Mack Bolan passed easily through the combined East and West German Intelligence units cleaning up the confusion at the Leipzig Fair. Most of the people around him didn't know his cover ID, but they gave him a wide berth. No mention was made of the Russian agents who had faded into the background awaiting retrieval.

He'd talked to Brognola a few minutes before. The big Fed was happy. The President was happy. Even the German government appeared to be satisfied in spite of the countless subterfuges that had taken place within German borders.

There was only one person left to talk to.

He found her standing by an abandoned arcade game with toy prizes clinging to the plywood walls. Her left arm was in a sling, and her coat was thrown loosely over her shoulders.

"How bad is it?" he asked, referring to the arm.

She shook her head, smiling up at him. Her eyes held pain, and something more. Straw clung to her hair. "Nothing permanent," she said. "In a few weeks, except for the scar, it'll be like nothing ever happened."

"I heard you took Perbandt down."

She arched her eyebrow at him. "Maybe I learned more than he thought I did. Maybe he wasn't as good as I thought he was."

"Could be. And now what happens?"

"Depends on your people," Falkenhayn said.

Bolan smiled. "You're a hero. The sky's the limit."

"I'm free to go?"

"Yeah."

She looked into his eyes. "You were wrong about me, you know."

Bolan said nothing.

"I'm not a believer. I'm a dreamer. I thought I could be part of something that could put everything right with the world."

"That's not a bad dream," the warrior said gently. "But it's a fool's dream if you think a handful of people can get the job done. If world peace is ever going to be achieved, it's going to take just that—the world."

"I know. You're a dreamer, too. I see that in you now. That's what touched us back there in the apartment." She paused, reaching out to touch his face with her fingers. "If things were different, if *you* were different, I'd want to see what the future held for us." She drew her hand away and tucked it into her pocket. "But you can't lay the gun down, can you?"

"No."

"There's a softness in you, a gentleness few are ever going to see. You're going to be remembered for that damn gun."

"I saw that for me a long time ago, Firenze. It's something I can't walk away from."

"Even if you wanted to?"

"No."

"Well, I can." She laid the .22 in his palm. "I'm tired of playing these deadly little games. I'm going to find a nice corner of the world somewhere and find out what's inside myself. Maybe, after a while, I'll discover something I can like about myself again."

"You will." Bolan dropped the little pistol in a pocket of his trench coat, then reached up to a wall of the game stand and took down a small stuffed bear. He gave it to her and said, "Somebody to keep you company until somebody better comes along. It won't be long at all."

She stuck the bear inside her sling, then used her free arm to wrap around his neck and pull him down to her. She kissed him, long and hard, her lips hot against his. Then she broke away. "Goodbye."

"Goodbye." Bolan watched her leave, a small shape fading into the darkness surrounding the fairgrounds.

She never looked back.

THE FREEDOM TRILOGY

Join Mack Bolan's fight for freedom in the freedom trilogy...

Beginning in June 1993, Gold Eagle presents a special three-book in-line continuity featuring Mack Bolan, the Executioner, along with ABLE TEAM and PHOENIX FORCE, as they face off against a communist dictator. A dictator with far-reaching plans to gain control of the troubled Baltic state area and whose ultimate goal is world supremacy. The fight for freedom starts in June with THE EXECUTIONER #174: Battle Plan, continues in THE EXECUTIONER #175: Battle Ground, and concludes in August with the longer 352-page Mack Bolan novel Battle Force.

Available at your favorite retail outlets in
June through to August.

FT93-1

Follow the exploits of a crack direct-action unit in the thrilling new miniseries from Gold Eagle...

by DAN MATTHEWS

The President just unleashed the big guns in the toughest offensive of the war on drugs—SLAM, the ultrasecret three-man strike team whose mandate is to search-locate-annihilate the threat posed by multinational drug conspiracies.

In Book 1: **FORCE OPTION,** a dangerous Mexican-Colombian axis forged by two drug kingpins ranks priority one for the SLAM team—a team that extracts payment with hot lead.

A new age of terrorism
calls for a new breed of hero

NOMAD

S M A R T   B O M B

D A V I D   A L E X A N D E R

**Code name: Nomad. He is the supreme fighting
machine, a new breed of elite commando
whose specialty is battling 21st-century
techno-terrorism with bare-knuckle combat
skills and state-of-the-art weapons.**

**Desperately racing against a lethal countdown,
Nomad tracks a rogue weapons expert but runs
into a trap. He comes face-to-face with his
hated nemesis in a deadly contest—a contest in
which the odds are stacked against him.**

Meet Jake Strait—a modern-day bounty hunter in the ruthless, anything-goes world of 2031.

by FRANK RICH

Jake Strait is a licensed enforcer in a world gone mad—a world where suburbs are guarded and farmlands are garrisoned around a city of evil.

In Book 1: **AVENGING ANGEL,** Jake Strait is caught in a maze of political deceit that will drench the city in a shower of spilled blood.